ABSOLUTE PERIL

(A JAKE MERCER POLITICAL THRILLER—BOOK 4)

JACK MARS

Jack Mars

Jack Mars is the USA Today bestselling author of the LUKE STONE thriller series, which includes seven books. He is also the author of the new FORGING OF LUKE STONE prequel series, comprising six books; of the AGENT ZERO spy thriller series, comprising twelve books; of the TROY STARK thriller series, comprising seven books; of the SPY GAME thriller series, comprising ten books; of the JAKE MERCER thriller series, comprising seven books (and counting); and of the new TYLER WOLF thriller series, comprising seven books (and counting).

Jack loves to hear from you, so please feel free to visit www.Jackmarsauthor.com to join the email list, receive a free book, receive free giveaways, connect on Facebook and Twitter, and stay in touch!

ISBN: 978-1-0943-8587-7

BOOKS BY JACK MARS

TYLER WOLF THRILLER SERIES
DOUBLE AGENT (Book #1)
DOUBLE CROSS (Book #2)
DOUBLE ASSET (Book #3)
DOUBLE DOCTRINE (Book #4)
DOUBLE JEOPARDY (Book #5)
DOUBLE THREAT (Book #6)
DOUBLE TARGET (Book #7)

JAKE MERCER THRILLER SERIES
ABSOLUTE THREAT (Book #1)
ABSOLUTE DAMAGE (Book #2)
ABSOLUTE FORCE (Book #3)
ABSOLUTE PERIL (Book #4)
ABSOLUTE TREASON (Book #5)
ABSOLUTE VENGEANCE (Book #6)
ABSOLUTE TARGET (Book #7)

THE SPY GAME
TARGET ONE (Book #1)
TARGET TWO (Book #2)
TARGET THREE (Book #3)
TARGET FOUR (Book #4)
TARGET FIVE (Book #5)
TARGET SIX (Book #6)
TARGET SEVEN (Book #7)
TARGET EIGHT (Book #8)
TARGET NINE (Book #9)
TARGET TEN (Book #10)

TROY STARK THRILLER SERIES
ROGUE FORCE (Book #1)
ROGUE COMMAND (Book #2)
ROGUE TARGET (Book #3)
ROGUE MISSION (Book #4)
ROGUE SHOT (Book #5)

ROGUE STRIKE (Book #6)
ROGUE ORDER (Book #7)

LUKE STONE THRILLER SERIES
ANY MEANS NECESSARY (Book #1)
OATH OF OFFICE (Book #2)
SITUATION ROOM (Book #3)
OPPOSE ANY FOE (Book #4)
PRESIDENT ELECT (Book #5)
OUR SACRED HONOR (Book #6)
HOUSE DIVIDED (Book #7)

FORGING OF LUKE STONE PREQUEL SERIES
PRIMARY TARGET (Book #1)
PRIMARY COMMAND (Book #2)
PRIMARY THREAT (Book #3)
PRIMARY GLORY (Book #4)
PRIMARY VALOR (Book #5)
PRIMARY DUTY (Book #6)

AN AGENT ZERO SPY THRILLER SERIES
AGENT ZERO (Book #1)
TARGET ZERO (Book #2)
HUNTING ZERO (Book #3)
TRAPPING ZERO (Book #4)
FILE ZERO (Book #5)
RECALL ZERO (Book #6)
ASSASSIN ZERO (Book #7)
DECOY ZERO (Book #8)
CHASING ZERO (Book #9)
VENGEANCE ZERO (Book #10)
ZERO ZERO (Book #11)
ABSOLUTE ZERO (Book #12)

PROLOGUE

"Christ, the smell. How do you stand it?"

Detective Matt Bachman moved his light slowly over the scene in front of him. The room did, in fact, smell terrible, though that had more to do with the alcohol stained… well, everything… then the body in the corner of the room between the bed and the far wall.

"You get used to it," he replied.

"I don't know if I want to get used to it," his partner, newly minted Detective Garrett Masters, replied.

"You do if you want to be a detective." Matt stepped into the room, noting the placement of various open containers of food, alcohol, and what he suspected would turn out to be prescription painkillers. No one knew how to live it up like politicians.

"I talked to Reception," Garrett said, reluctantly following Matt into the room. "The stiff is Al—"

"Victim."

"What?"

"The *victim*, not the stiff. This isn't a movie."

Garrett looked like he wanted to be irritated, but he knew better than to argue. "The *victim* is Albert Kline."

Matt turned to Garrett and lifted an eyebrow. "*The* Albert Kline?"

"One and the same. Chairman of the Horizon Group and CEO of Horizon Weapons Systems."

So not a politician, but damned close. Horizon was the largest supplier of ordnance in the country, and Albert no doubt had the entire national security council on speed dial.

Or he did, anyway.

"Too bad he didn't have one of those Diamondback missiles in his room," Garrett quipped. "That would have taken care of the attackers for sure." He grinned at Matt, but his smile faded quickly when it became clear that his partner didn't appreciate the joke.

"Looks like a robbery," Matt said, sweeping his flashlight at the overturned dresser drawers and scattered belongings. "But it isn't. Know how I can tell?"

"Because you're the god of detective work?"

Matt glared at his young partner. “You’re real funny today. A regular Johnny Carson.”

“Who?”

Matt stared in silence for a moment before turning away. "Jesus. Anyway, I'll bet you anything that his cash will be gone, along with a few token items from his belongings. But see that watch?" He shone his light on the Rolex still attached to Kline’s wrist. “That’s worth more than the rest of this room combined, and they left it.”

“Maybe they didn’t think they’d be able to sell it.”

“Nah, that’s not it. If they’re willing to murder a man for his belongings, they’ll take everything and figure out what’s worth something later. No, this was a murder, probably for hire.”

“Why for hire?”

“I don’t know yet. I just have a…”

He stopped when he saw something on the wall behind Kline’s body. He was about to say he had a hunch, but if that was what he thought it was, then his hunch was wrong.

It was what he thought it was.

“Forget what I said. This wasn’t a murder for hire. This was political.”

“Political? How do you—Oh.”

The two detectives stared at the symbol of a ring surrounding a three-pronged trident written in Kline’s blood on the wall.

“The good news,” Matt said, “is this is now officially out of our hands.”

He pulled his phone out of his pocket and made a call.

CHAPTER ONE

Senior Special Agent Jake Mercer of the United States Secret Service vaulted over the low rail, then slid under the high one. He brought his weapon up and fired twice in rapid succession. The plastic pellets impacted the bullseyes of the targets, and twin chimes sounded to indicate good hits.

Jake got quickly to his feet and rushed toward the door. He lowered his shoulder and crashed through, rolling and coming to a knee.

There were three targets in the room. One was a civilian. Jake quickly shot the bullseyes of the other two targets, then pushed the civilian target to the ground, shielding it with his body.

A target popped up as he lowered the civilian, and he quickly fired. The shot didn't land in the bullseye but did score inside the red kill ring outside.

Jake pushed down a flash of irritation and moved on through the course. After this building was an open square where five terrorists held civilians hostage. Targets on tracks popped up randomly, simulating vehicles and panicked civilians, and forcing Jake to take care with every shot.

He managed to stop all five terrorists without civilian casualties. As the last target fell, an alarm sounded, and the clock on the wall began to count down in red numbers.

Jake sprinted up an incline, weaving between obstacles and vaulting over others. The time ticked steadily down as he ran toward the target on the far end of the room. When the clock reached ten seconds, a gentle feminine voice began to count down. "Ten… nine… eight…"

"Yeah, yeah, I hear you," he muttered.

He picked up the pace, rushing for the target. Other targets popped up as he ran, and he shot three that were labeled terrorists, leaving two civilians unharmed.

"Three… two…"

He leapt onto the platform and slammed the red button just as the female voice said, "One…"

There was a brief pause, then the room's lights flashed blue before everything reset to the start position.

Jake walked in a circle around the platform with his hands on his head, catching his breath. His side wasn't hurting anymore, which was good. His knee wasn't spasming anymore, which was better.

But his cardio was still crap. He should have been able to complete that training session without being left so completely out of breath.

"Need a break, old man?"

He chuckled and turned to his partner, Special Agent Jess Foster. Jess wore her typical workout outfit of yoga pants and a combination sports bra/halter top. Both items clung tightly to the curves of her body, and Jake felt the usual touch of discomfort at that. Jess was a very attractive woman, but he was in love with Sheila, and even though he knew it was foolish, he couldn't help but feel a little guilty each time he noticed how fit his partner was.

She tossed him a water bottle and said, "Since you didn't answer me, I'm going to assume that you do need a break."

"Actually, I'm done for the day."

"Really? Already?"

"Screw you. I've been here for three hours."

"That's your problem."

She took a sip of her water and leaned against the wall in front of him. "How was it?"

"How was what?"

"The workout, dumbass. How do you feel?"

"Old and out of shape."

At thirty-five, Jake wasn't the fresh-faced kid who finished top of his unit in boot camp, but he was far from old. The exhaustion and slowed response time were an effect of several protracted recoveries from injuries sustained in his past few assignments.

But he still felt old and out of shape.

"Good!" Jess said, "So normal."

He rolled his eyes. "You're only eight years younger than me. Don't get cocky. It'll catch up to you."

Jess giggled. "Seriously, though, how are you feeling?"

"I'm good. The side's all right, and my knees aren't barking yet. I'm just slow and more out of breath than I should be after a little training session."

"Some would say that you should be out of breath after a training session, or you're not really working hard."

"Whatever. You know what I mean."

"I know you're a grump who can't bring himself to have a positive thought. Seriously, think of how sexy you would have looked for Sheila if she were here. That should cheer you up."

"You think I look sexy?"

"I'm not going to answer that, because I feel like if I do, you'll turn it into some lame joke. If there's anything you should be ashamed of, it's your sense of humor."

Jake chuckled. "Well, we're Secret Service agents. We're not supposed to be funny. You're the weird one, not me."

"I'll cop to that. Are you going to drink that water, or are you planning on collecting your sweat and drinking that instead?"

"On second thought, maybe you are a real agent."

She rolled her eyes and swiped at the water bottle, taking it and sipping gratefully. When she was done, she asked, "Have you talked to Art yet?"

"No, why?"

She shook her head. "You need to convince Sheila to give you some time to talk to the other people in your life."

"I only see Sheila once a week."

"Then you need to make time to talk to the other people in your life."

"I see you every day."

She rolled her eyes. "Well, if you had seen your boss, he probably would have told you that we're assigned to the President's personal security detail next week."

Jake's brow furrowed. "Why? What happened to Dawson?"

"Nothing. He's taking the same week off. I'm joining the detail because of my unparalleled expertise in electronic warfare, communications and monitoring and pretty much everything having to do with technology."

"They want you onboard in case Trident tries to short out Air Force One?"

"Yeah, basically. You're going because the President requested you specifically."

"Bryan requested me?"

"Yep. He seems to feel his family's safest when you're the one protecting them. That's good news, right? For you and Sheila, I mean. He's coming around."

"Yeah, I suppose you're right."

"I'm always right." She took another sip of water, then asked, "Have you heard about Kline?"

"Kline? Who's Kline?"

"The defense contractor who just got murdered."

"Oh, Albert Kline. I thought you meant someone in the Service."

"No, I mean the subject of every news story that's been aired since last night. Do you now watch the news?"

"Not while I'm working out."

"What time do you go to bed? Ten?"

"Yeah, so?"

She stared at him incredulously. "My God, you *are* old. Well, anyway, Albert Kline was murdered in his hotel room after a party with a bunch of other defense contractors and government officials."

"That so?"

"Yep. A few things were stolen, but the FBI doesn't think it's a robbery."

"The FBI? Why are they involved? Do they think this is politically motivated?"

"Well, they found the Trident logo written in blood next to his body."

Jake's eyes snapped to hers. "What?"

"Yep. That's why the FBI is involved."

Trident was a terrorist organization headed by former Secret Service agent Eli Bard and former Marine Andrew McNeill. In the past year, they had been responsible for nearly a dozen attacks on the President and caused the deaths of hundreds of civilians. It had been nearly four months since Jake had heard anything from them. If they were back now, then the peace he had enjoyed would soon be shattered.

"Are they sure it's Trident and not someone trying to throw them off the scent?"

"No, they're not. Actually, right now, they're pretty sure it's the second one. Kline had a lot of enemies: business, government and personal. The FBI is thinking that one of them tried to throw Trident under the bus."

"What do you think?"

"I think it's odd. They murdered Kline, staged it as a robbery—staged it badly, I might add—then painted Trident's logo in Kline's blood on the wall. It's just odd."

Jake frowned. If there was a chance that this was Trident, then he should be investigating this. Art could handpick a team that could handle the President's protection just as well as Jake could.

He wouldn't admit it to Jess, but part of his zeal was personal. He hadn't known Bard well, but Drew was once Jake's best friend. The two of them had served as a team in the Marine Corps, fighting in four different countries before their final engagement resulted in a court martial that saw Drew demoted and dishonorably discharged. Their friendship had ended then, but Jake would never have suspected Drew of joining a terrorist group.

But he had. Jake had seen Drew kill innocent people. He was a terrorist, a murderer, and a traitor to his country, and if he had ever been the man Jake thought he was, he had lost that man along the way and would never get him back.

"Hey. Earth to Jake. You still with me?"

"Yeah. I was just thinking that if this is Trident, then we should be investigating this ourselves and letting someone else handle the security detail."

"Well, the President *did* ask for you personally."

"I can tell him that I'm needed on the Trident investigation. Any number of agents are qualified to handle security. If Dawson's taking time off, Trent or Merrill can handle it. Hell, Art can handpick a team. We should be looking for Bard and Drew."

Jess smiled softly at him. "I get it. I want these assholes as badly as you do. But it's probably not them. This was an amateur job, and not a good one. They're trying to hide behind Trident, but it's far too poorly executed to be something Bard is involved in."

Jake sighed. "Yeah, you're probably right."

"I'm always right. I thought we covered that."

"So Bryan said it has to be me, huh?"

"Actually, Sheila did," Jess replied. "No surprise there."

Bryan Jackson was the President of the United States. He was also a friend of Jake's. Jake wasn't sure if he was still a friend or not. Jake's girlfriend, Sheila, happened to be Bryan's daughter, and Bryan wasn't happy with their relationship. He had good reasons for that. After all, Jake was supposed to have no conflicts of interest when it came to his duty, and having a romantic relationship with one of the people he was charged to protect was as conflicting of an interest as it got.

Jake suspected the real reason had more to do with his volatile past and the violent nature of his work. That was also a good reason.

But he loved Sheila, and she loved him. The two of them had tried to deny their feelings, but that hadn't worked well for either of them. So, they were together, and while the President no longer actively opposed the relationship, he made no attempt to hide his feelings about it.

"Got it. Well, I hope she's not expecting too much fun. I'll be working the entire trip."

"That's a you-and-Sheila conversation, buddy. I'm not touching that with a six-thousand-millimeter pole."

Jake laughed. "You're such a dork, Jess."

"I'm still not touching it. If you're not careful, though, I'll touch you."

"What? Hey!" He narrowly avoided the kick Jess aimed at his leg. "What the hell?"

"Come on, old man," Jess said as she laced up some MMA gloves. "Let's spar."

"You want to have a sparring match with me?"

"I mean, it's not going to be much of a match, but I'm going to enjoy kicking your butt."

He chuckled again and said, "I'm not going to fight you. That's… hey!"

She feinted with a jab, then swept his left foot. He stumbled backwards, barely keeping his feet. Jess giggled and said, "Come on! Fight back, or it's going to look even worse."

"You realize I was a Marine, right."

"That was a long, long, long, long, long, hey!"

While she teased him, he rushed her, sliding under her counterpunch and wrapping her in a wrestling hold. She struggled in his arms, but he held her tightly. "You gonna behave?"

She glared playfully back at him and said, "You could have at least let me win for a few minutes."

"Um… hello?"

Jake and Jess looked up to see Sheila standing a few feet away, frowning at them. Jake quickly released Jess, who stammered. "Sorry. We were sparring. We, um… just training."

Jake rolled his eyes. *Way to make it not awkward at all, Jess.*

Sheila nodded once, slowly. "I see. Should I come back later?"

"No," Jess and Jake said at the same time. Jake frowned at Jess, who decided she was very interested in retying her shoes.

"No," Jake repeated. "We were just finished."

Sheila kept her eyes on Jess and said, "Well, I was going to see if you wanted to grab breakfast, but if you have other plans…"

"No other plans. Breakfast sounds great. I need to stop by my apartment to shower and change, though. I'm sweaty."

Sheila gave him a fishy look. "Hmm." She looked pointedly at Jess. "I'll go with you."

"Yep," Jake said. "Sounds good."

He walked to Sheila and put her arm around her, steering her away from the red-faced Jess, who just couldn't get enough of her darned shoelaces.

He kept his attention on Sheila as they drove to his apartment, but his thoughts kept turning to the fake Trident killing. He wanted to believe that Jess was right, and this was an amateur outfit just trying to hide behind a more well-known group, but he couldn't help but wonder if this was yet another of Bard's convoluted plans.

Either way, he had a bad feeling that this flight wasn't going to be a smooth one.

CHAPTER TWO

"Sir?"

"What is it, Coulson?" Jake asked without looking up from the panel he was inspecting.

Special Agent David Coulson was the youngest agent on board, although at twenty-nine, he was only seven years younger than Jake himself. He came with seven years of exemplary experience in the agency, however, and was personally recommended for the mission by Jake's boss, Deputy Director Arthur Davis.

"The President wants to know how much longer." Coulson said.

"As long as it takes," Jake replied. "Air Force One isn't leaving the tarmac until and unless I confirm that there's no sign of terrorist activity."

"Yes, sir, but…"

Jake sighed and stood, turning to face the junior agent. "But?"

"Well, I can't tell him that, sir."

"Yes, you can. And you have to. Your job is to keep the President safe. That will sometimes mean telling him things he doesn't want to hear. You need to be willing to ignore and even disobey the President's instructions if it's necessary to keep him safe."

"Yes, sir," Coulson agreed. "Shall I tell the same thing to the crew?"

"The crew? They're impatient too?"

Coulson shrugged. "They just asked me to talk to you."

Jake sighed and rubbed his temples. He hoped this wasn't going to be a thing for long. The old crew understood Jake and his priorities. New crews sometimes had difficulty understanding that their schedule was subordinate to the President's safety. Well, that wasn't entirely true. They just didn't understand that sometimes, actual threats to the President's safety occurred. Somehow, even after the year they'd had, people just couldn't believe that serious threats existed from serious terrorists.

"Go and tell everyone who asks that I will personally inform them when the plane is safe to board. If they haven't heard from me, then the answer is not yet. Got it?"

"Yes, sir," Coulson replied, a little wounded. He headed back out of the airplane, and Jake and the other senior agents continued their inspection. Fortunately for the impatient people waiting outside, he was nearly finished when Coulson interrupted him, and ten minutes later, the passengers entered the vehicle.

Bryan greeted Jake with a curt nod, and Jake returned an equally curt nod of his own. Carrie, the President's wife and Sheila's mother, glared at him, making no attempt to hide her disdain. If Bryan was ambivalent about his daughter's relationship with Jake, Carrie was actively and bitterly opposed.

The next passenger was Sheila. She and Jess were chatting and laughing together as they boarded. Watching the two of them walk onto the plane, Jake couldn't help but compare the two. Both were stunningly beautiful, but while Jess was toned and athletic and had brown eyes and straight black hair that stopped just below her shoulder blades, Sheila was slender and feminine with wavy blonde hair that framed her face and contrasted beautifully with her soft blue eyes.

She smiled at Jake when she walked on board, and Jake fell in love with her all over again.

The last passenger was the President's personal assistant, a rather harried young man named Derek whose eyes never left the tablet from which he managed the President's every moment. Bryan had grudgingly agreed to hire an assistant after the White House Chief of Staff had implored him to let someone else manage his schedule so the President didn't continue to do foolish things like travel to the location of a planned terrorist attack out of some misguided sense of bravado.

Once everyone was on board, Jake did a final check of the plane, then introduced himself to the flight crew. He had reviewed their personnel files before, but other agents had handled the background checks and Secret Service interviews.

Three passengers. four crew. Nine Secret Service agents, including Jake and Jess.

"All right," Jake said to the gathered crew. "You've all been briefed, so I won't take up too much of your time. I'll just remind everyone present that the safety of the President and his family takes top priority. I am in charge of their safety, and that means I am in charge of what happens on board this aircraft. Captain Sontag, you are the aircraft commander, and if there's a safety issue, you are, of course, free to make the call to divert, but you are not free to override or ignore any of my instructions unless there is a safety issue that prevents you from complying. The same goes for everyone else in the cockpit. If I say we divert and land somewhere else, we divert and land somewhere else. If I say we stay in the air, we stay in the air. This is not now, nor will it ever be, up for discussion. Do you understand?"

The crew voiced their understanding, and Jake said, "Excellent. If at any time, there is a safety issue of any kind, mechanical or otherwise, I need to be made aware of it as soon as possible. Is that clear?"

The crew echoed their agreement.

"Outstanding. Does anyone have anything they need to discuss before the flight takes off?" After a moment of silence, Jake said, "Wonderful. Let's have a safe flight."

The crew dispersed, and Jake headed back to the main cabin. He expected it to contain only Jess and Special Agent Coulson, but when he entered, he saw Sheila and her two assigned agents, Trent and Merrill, sitting in the jumpseats that were normally folded along the wall.

She smiled at him and waved him over, patting the seat next to her. He hesitated, but he didn't have any immediately pressing business, so he sat next to her.

"Hey, baby," she said, kissing his cheek and stroking his hair. "How have you been?"

"I'm well, ma'am," he said stiffly.

She rolled her eyes. "Come on, Jake. Everyone knows we're together. There's no need to be so forma."

"I'm on duty, ma'am. It's important that I conduct myself properly."

She sighed and shook her head. "Very well. Whatever you need to tell yourself." She took her hand from his head but left it on his lap. "I'm going to touch you if I want to, though." Her eyes twinkled. "That's an order."

He just managed to keep from cracking a smile. "Yes, ma'am."

"Ooh, I like this ma'am thing," Sheila teased. "Jess, does he ever call you ma'am?"

"Only when I'm bossing him around," Jess called back. She sat at a small desk and watched her laptop screen for any sign of electromagnetic threat.

"Maybe I'll boss you around tonight," Sheila teased, whispering in Jake's ear. "Would you like that?"

He sighed. "Sheila, please. I need to be professional."

Trent and Merrill exchanged a look. Merrill smiled slightly, and Trent nodded, then turned to Sheila. "Ma'am, would you and Special Agent Mercer like some privacy?"

"No," Jake said, "You two—"

"Yes, please," Sheila said. "Thank you."

"Of course, ma'am," Trent replied. He turned to Jake and saluted crisply, struggling to keep from letting his smile show. "We'll be in our bunks if you need us, sir."

"Trent, Merrill, you two are ordered to remain by—"

Sheila pulled his face to her and kissed him deeply. He tried to pull away, but she held him still, and rather than be forceful with her, he just resigned himself to dealing with it.

Not that it was hard for him to accept a passionate kiss from the woman he loved.

Sheila pulled away after a moment, and said, "See? Relax and have fun, Jake. We're on vacation. You're here because I wanted to spend time with you. Let your employees handle the safety part. We'll be fine!"

"I would like to point out that I'm not an employee," Jess said, "I'm his partner."

"And you have our safety under control, right?"

"I do."

"So he can stop acting like a worry wart and enjoy himself for once, right?"

"He sure can."

"Awesome. Jake, enjoy yourself and stop acting like a worry wart for once."

Jake sighed and shook his head. "You two are going to be the death of me."

"Death at the hands of two beautiful women is a great way to go," Sheila pointed out. She took his hand in hers and said, "Come on, babe. Let's just pretend we're a normal couple for once."

He looked at her and saw the love she had for him radiating from her smile. Behind that, though, he saw the pleading in her eyes. She needed this. She needed to feel like everything was normal and the two of them were just like any other couple.

Sheila, understandably, had a hard time dealing with the fact that her father was the target of a terrorist organization. She had been present for several of the attacks and was keenly aware of how many had died, keeping her and her family safe. She had confided in Jake that when her father was no longer President, she hoped to retire to a small home in a rural area somewhere far from D.C. She dreamed of a quiet, normal life and hoped that Jake would join her.

Jake had done little to reassure her of that future. With Bard and Drew still at large, and his duty to the President still paramount, he hadn't allowed himself to think of what would happen when Bard and Drew were in custody, Trident was disbanded, and Bryan was no longer President.

But she needed this fantasy now. Even if she knew it wasn't real, she needed it now. He sighed and said, "All right. I'll do my best."

She grinned and kissed him again, softly this time. "Thank you."

The engines roared as the plane began its takeoff roll. Most of the roar was muffled by the extra insulation of Air Force One, but Jake could still sense the fury of the powerful turbofan engines as they lifted the massive plane airborne.

"Here we go!" Sheila said brightly. "Hey, Jake, can you help me with something in my cabin really quickly?"

She gave Jake a devilish grin, and Jake felt heat climb his cheeks. "Sheila, I really—"

"I'll call you if we need anything, Jake," Jess interrupted. "Go help her out."

She kept her eyes on her screen, but Jake could see the smile playing on her lips.

"Thank you, Jess," he said drily. "You're a big help."

"Anything for you, buddy," she said.

Sheila led Jake to her cabin, closing and locking the door behind them. The cabin was, of course, quite small. It contained a twin-size bunk, a small table with a chair and a lamp, and a shower/toilet combo. Normally, it would be occupied by the National Security Advisor, but since this was a family trip, Sheila was using it.

"Sheila, we can't do this," Jake said. "I'm working."

"Well, I'm not," Sheila said, reaching back and unbuttoning her dress. "I'm on vacation with my boyfriend, and I'm going to enjoy every second of that vacation." She let the dress fall, and Jake's protests died on his lips. "And so are you."

She went to him, and Jake finally let go of his reservations and allowed himself to enjoy a moment of peace with the woman he loved.

CHAPTER THREE

"Ladies and gentlemen, this is your captain speaking. We have reached our cruising altitude of forty-five thousand feet. That should keep us above the commercial flights and above any turbulence we might face along the way. We are *flying against the jet stream, so this flight will take a little longer than normal. We're looking at touching down in Honolulu in about nine and a half hours. Thank you."*

Trent chuckled. "Aren't first-timers cute?"

"I don't know," Merrill replied. "Hey, Coulson, do you feel cute?"

Coulson smiled and lifted his middle finger up to the more senior agent. Merrill laughed and said, "At least they haven't tried to blow the plane up."

"That's not funny," Jake said, casting a stern look at Merrill.

"Come on, Jake. We have to be stone-faced all the time. Let us enjoy a little levity."

"There's a time and place for that, Merrill. Forty-five thousand feet in the air guarding the President and his family isn't that time or place."

Trent smiled slyly at Jake. "You sure you want to talk about time and place, Romeo?" Jake's scowl deepened, and Trent lifted his hands placatingly. "Joking. Joking. But also, kind of not. Relax, boss man. We're good. We went over every inch of this plane and every inch of its crew with a fine-toothed comb."

"I'll bet you did," Coulson said. "I saw you going over every inch of that sexy first officer."

"I did, and I'm not ashamed. She should be named Melina stone-cold Fox."

"Nobody says that anymore."

"I do."

Jake left the three agents to joke around. It wasn't all that inappropriate of them to joke around while they were on break, but Jake wasn't in the mood for it. He thought that reaching cruising altitude without incident would ease his worries, but that didn't seem to be the case.

He walked to the main cabin, where Jess remained at her chair, sitting across from the President, his wife and his daughter. The on-duty agents wore appropriately emotionless expressions and nodded formally at Jake as he entered.

"Jake," Bryan said cheerfully. "We were just talking about you."

"Good things, I hope, sir."

"Well, it was your partner speaking, so the most horrible things you can think of."

"Yep," Jess concerned. "I went deep into the vault for the most horrible things I could possibly share."

Jake managed a mile as he took a seat next to Jess. "I'll have to work to overcome whatever damage Jess has done to my reputation."

Bryan laughed. "Jake, will you relax? God, Sheila was right. You're so tense."

"Seriously," Sheila agreed. "It's like dating a steel rod."

She winked at Jake, and Jake felt heat climb his cheeks again at the innuendo. He lifted his eyes to the First Lady and wasn't surprised to see her staring daggers at her. She looked at her husband and said, "Honey, can we return to our cabin? I'm feeling a little tired."

"You can go on, I'll meet you in a few minutes."

She frowned. "You said we could watch a movie together."

"We will. A few minutes is a few minutes, babe. I'll be there soon."

Carrie glanced over at Jake, and Jake was grateful that she didn't have the ability to conjure his death from a distance. She looked at her daughter and almost pleaded, "Will you keep me company, Sheila?"

Sheila hesitated and glanced at Jake. Jake shook his head slightly, hoping Carrie wouldn't see the movement.

She did. Her face flamed, and her lips pressed into a thin line, but she said nothing. Sheila got Jake's point and stood. "Sure, I'll go with you. I actually feel kind of tired myself. I'll see you in a few, Dad." She looked at Jake and said, "Bye, babe. Love you," then looked pointedly at her mother.

Carrie scoffed but didn't say anything as she walked ahead of her daughter to the President's stateroom. Bryan's smile had faded, and his shoulders were bunched slightly. Jess turned to her computer and pretended to be busy with something. The four agents in the room remained stock still and stoic.

"Well, that was fun," Bryan finally said, breaking the silence. "So Jake, how have you been? I haven't seen you since the day after Hadad tried to blow up the Memorial Lawn. How are your wounds treating you?"

"They're all right, sir, thank you," Jake said. "I've been cleared for duty."

Bryan sighed. "Jake, you don't have to be so formal, okay? I appreciate it, but I'm talking to you as a friend now. How are you?"

Jake thought a moment before replying. Bryan might be his friend, but he was always the President, and there was no such thing as permission to speak freely. "Are we friends?"

Well, he tried to think before replying, anyway.

Bryan frowned and tensed slightly. "I think we are. Do you feel differently?"

Jake sighed. "I feel like you're… well, it feels like you're unhappy with me, sir."

"Bryan."

"Bryan. It feels like you're unhappy with me. I'm not sure if it's because we're at odds with each other over how to handle the Trident threat or because you resent my relationship with Sheila, but to be honest, I wasn't sure that we *were* friends anymore."

Bryan sighed. "I'm not going to pretend I'm happy with you dating my daughter, but it isn't because I think you're beneath her, and it's not because I think you're compromising yourself by allowing a conflict of interest. The reality is that you two want different lives. Maybe that will change in the future, but right now, it's hard to see either of you compromising. I didn't want to talk about that right now, though. I just wanted to hang out. Believe it or not, I get tired of constantly being on the job too. Sheila was the one who asked you to join us, but I agreed because I hoped that you and I could bridge the gap between us too."

Jake looked around at the others in the room. The four bodyguards were doing an outstanding job of pretending to be statues. They were good agents. Jess was doing a much poorer job of pretending to be engrossed in whatever she was looking at on her computer screen. Jake sighed and said, "Sir—Bryan, I don't feel like there's a gap between us. I feel like there's a wall. I want…" he thought how to phrase this. "Your safety is paramount, Bryan. Not just because it's you, and not just because you're the President."

"Because of Sheila. I understand."

"No, you don't." Far too much frustration had crept into his voice, even for a casual conversation, but Jake couldn't stifle it anymore. "Your safety is paramount because the Office of the Presidency must remain strong. All Presidents must be kept safe because we need a sitting President to be able to guide the nation through times of fear and darkness. You've been behaving as though the way to show strength is to ignore threats or not take them seriously, but that's foolish. That doesn't show strength, that shows stubbornness."

Jess gasped and tried to disguise it with a cough. Bryan's eyes narrowed, and for a moment, Jake was certain that he'd gone too far. Then Bryan said, "I've compromised on that point. I no longer fly to locales with high risks of imminent terrorist attack, and I have a full contingent of bodyguards everywhere I go. What I can't do is hide in Camp David until Trident is brought to justice. I can't run the country from a bunker."

"I understand, sir," Jake said. "I'm not asking for that. I'm only asking that you not take unnecessary risks."

The cabin door opened, and Sierra the flight attendant walked in. She flinched when she saw Jake there and stuttered a little when she turned to the President. "Sir? Will you be taking your dinner here or in your stateroom?"

"My stateroom, thank you," the President said. He stood and, to Jake's surprise, extended his hand. Jake took it, and Bryan said, "I know I'm a lot to put up with. Thank you for hanging in there. I promise you, when I leave the White House, I'll spend the rest of my life living on a farm in Kentucky. I'll never make a public appearance again."

Jake chuckled and said, "I'll hold you to that, sir."

"Sheila will hold us *both* to that," Bryan said.

He released Jake's hand and allowed the nervous Sierra to escort him from the room. Just before she left, she turned to Jake and regarded him with an odd expression before following the President. The four bodyguards were the last to leave. One of them, Special Agent Patel, caught Jake's eye before he left and mimed tugging on his collar. Jake smiled slightly and decided not to reprimand the agent. Protocol, evidently, was not going to be all that rigid on this flight.

Jake's smile faded as he thought of the look the flight attendant gave him. If it had been a nervous look, he wouldn't have thought twice about it, but it wasn't. It was almost… calculating.

He turned to Jess to see his partner staring at him wide-eyed. "You saw it too?"

"What, you and Bryan having an actual conversation? Like people? I know, right? Buy your lottery tickets today, folks."

Jake rolled his eyes. "I meant the flight attendant. Did you notice how she looked at me?"

Jess sighed. “Okay. I hate that I’m the one who has to tell you this, Jake, but you’re a good-looking guy. Women are going to look at you, even though you’re taken.”

"That didn't seem like an attraction to me."

“That’s because you’re a man. Men don’t know how to tell when women are attracted to them because we don’t shamelessly ogle men we like. Trust me, Sierra thinks you’re cute. She’s not an idiot. She won’t try anything, but she’ll look because you’re worth looking at. To her. Not to me. I like men who smile every now and then.”

Jake frowned. “If you say so. It looked more like she was sizing me up.”

“You mean looking you up and down? Taking the view in?”

“Okay,” he said, lifting his hands. “I get it. There’s no need to—”

“Excuse me, sir.”

Jake turned to see Special Agent Roberts approaching with a frown. The frown didn’t worry Jake too much—Roberts was a serious type—but the item Roberts held in his hand worried Jake considerably. It was a small digital timer, the kind that people used when cooking.

Or when they planned on detonating a bomb.

“Where did you find that?”

“In the President’s bathroom, sir. It didn’t seem to be attached to anything, but I thought Jess could take a look at it and see if there was an antenna of some sort. It could be harmless, but...”

“But we’re going to make sure,” Jake finished. “Jess, can you—"

Before he could finish, the lights flickered. An alarm went off in Jake’s head. He tapped his radio and said, “Patel. Status now.”

Silence.

“Dammit.”

He and Roberts rushed from the room, gun drawn. Just before they reached the President’s stateroom, Patel left and lifted a hand for Jake to stop. “All clear, sir,” he said quietly. “Radios are down, but the President and his family are safe.”

“Who’s in the room besides you three and the family?”

“Just us, sir. Mr. Trumbull will arrive with dinner soon. Would you prefer I take it outside the room?”

“Yes. I want you three with the President at all times. Roberts, join them. I’m bringing the other three back from break and stationing them at the galley, the cockpit and Sheila’s cabin. I don’t know what just happened, but—”

The door to the cockpit opened, and Dana Porter—the relief captain—smiled and approached the two of them. "It looks like you two figured out the radio issue. The captain didn't want to alarm anyone, so he sent me out to talk to you. At this time, it appears that only onboard communications are affected. We still have contact with air traffic control as well as Air Force communication."

"What happened?" Jake asked.

"We're guessing an electrical short. Franz and I are going to investigate."

"An electrical short wouldn't have impacted our radios."

Dana blinked. Then her eyes widened. "Wait. You don't think we're being jammed, do you?"

"I don't know, but you should take my partner with you. She's an expert with technology."

She nodded, her eyes as wide as saucers. "Okay. I mean, yes, sir."

"I'll send Jess to the cockpit to meet you."

"Of course, sir."

Jake returned to the main cabin to get Jess. He would send Coulson with her too. Just in case.

When he reached Jess, she gave him a sober look. "Bad news, Jake."

Jake frowned. "What is it?"

"We've lost outgoing communications as well."

CHAPTER FOUR

Jake's frown deepened into a scowl. "Completely?"

"I'll let you know in a moment."

She sat down at her laptop and started pressing keys. He frowned. "How is your laptop still working?"

"It's in a shielded case hardened against EM pulses. I guess if you held it up to the jamming pod on an EA-18, you could probably fry it, but short of that, it's hard to break through."

"Why don't they do that with Air Force One?"

She pointed at the case, which was about three inches thick and appeared to be solid metal. "Because this is twenty pounds of lead to protect a five-pound laptop. Scale that up and you start running into problems like not being able to leave the ground."

"Got it. Well, I'm just glad it's still working."

"Me too."

While she worked, Jake walked to the cockpit. The four flight crew wore the same ashen faces. Jake frowned at Captain Sontag and said, "I'm now being told we lost outgoing communications. When did this happen?"

"Umm, a few minutes ago," Captain Sontag replied. "I was trying to reboot comms to see if that would fix it before I bothered you with it."

"From now on, I know everything that happens the moment it happens, understand?"

"Yes, sir."

"Good." He looked at Dana. "I'm keeping my partner with me. She's going to see if she can find an outside source."

"How is she going to do that with no communication to the outside world?"

"Don't worry about it. You keep looking for an inside source. You see anything out of the ordinary, I know about it immediately. Understand?"

"Yes. You got it."

Jake held her gaze a moment longer, then returned to the main cabin. When he arrived, he motioned Coulson close and said softly. "I want the President and his family secured in his stateroom. Three men in the room, two at the doorway, one at the cockpit and one at the galley. No one gets in or out but the President, his family, or one of us. No flight crew, no cabin crew, understand? Just so we're clear, the President *cannot* overrule that instruction."

Coulson definitely didn't look comfortable at being told to defy the President, but he nodded. "Understood, sir."

Jake turned to Jess, who regarded him with a sober look. "No good. I can't get through either."

Jake shook his head. "It has to be sabotage, then. Your laptop has its own transmitter, right?"

"Yes. To be fair, I can't be certain that it's sabotage. A lot of the wiring in this plane is old. That's why they're replacing them with the VC-25Bs next year."

"How does the plane's wiring result in a loss of satellite communications for your laptop?"

"Well, the issue is that the frequency switch is locked. Well, the switch itself isn't locked, but the switch isn't communicating to the dial—the actual one inside the radio."

"Okay, just the meat and potatoes," Jake said. "What's wrong?"

"The radio is creating a static field that's making our communications unlistenable. Essentially, Air Force One is jamming itself. I'm not ruling out sabotage, but the state of the wiring harness is suspect."

"So the President of the United States is on an aircraft that isn't suitable for transporting passengers?"

"You'll have to talk to the Air Force about that. Technically, the problem might not have seemed serious. You know how you'll hear an engine noise and you know you have to deal with it later, but you don't want to spend five grand on it right now?"

"Yeah, this is Air Force One. There's no later." He sighed and said, "All right. We're turning around. If the radio is jamming us with static, then people can see us, right?"

"Oh yeah. We're the brightest thing on every radar screen within two hundred miles."

"Then they'll at least see us coming. We're turning around, and we're landing at the nearest U.S. military airfield. The President will be transferred to the other VC-25A with an entirely different crew."

He headed to the cockpit and knocked on the door. Trent was already there guarding the door. "Everything okay?" he asked Jake.

“I’ll let you know.” Jake knocked again. “Captain? This is Special Agent Mercer. I need to talk to you.”

The door opened, and the First Officer ushered Jake in. Melina’s face was ashen, but she did a decent job of keeping her composure. “Captain, it’s Special Agent Mercer.”

“Thank you, Melina. Would you mind closing the door?”

As soon as the door was closed, Captain Sontag turned to Jake. “I haven’t announced this yet, but with our satellite communications out, we also don’t have GPS.”

“So we’re flying blind?”

"Not completely. I still have sonar, which gives me a decent idea of the terrain below. We have backup systems for navigation that can give me a rough estimate of our position, but we're flying like it's fifty years ago. We can still get to Honolulu, but—"

“No. We’re turning around right now. We’re heading to the nearest U.S. military airfield, and the President and his family are debarking immediately. I don’t know for sure that this is sabotage, but I’m not taking any risks.”

Sontag glanced at Melina, and Jake’s eyes narrowed. “Do we have a problem, Captain?” he asked, his voice low and deadly.

Sontag handed Jake his tablet. “We received that message out of the blue just before the radio went out. I copied it there.”

Jake looked at the message, and a chill ran through him.

STAY THE COURSE. THE PRESIDENT MUST PROCEED TO HAWAII.

It was fairly innocuous in and of itself, but considering the circumstances that followed immediately after, it could easily be construed as a threat.

The question was, did they follow the instructions or ignore them?

“What would you like us to do, sir?”

Jake thought, but no answer presented itself. He could order the plane to turn around, but he had no idea who had sabotaged the plane or what else they might be capable of. He could be ordering everyone on board to their doom.

“How long until we reach Hawaii?”

“Seven hours.”

“How long until we’re over the Pacific?”

“Two hours.”

“All right. Keep heading that way for now. I’m going to scour the plane for any sign of a threat, and we’ll proceed from there.”

"Didn't you do that already?" Melina asked.

"I did. But I'm also going to order every single crew member—including you—to take a seat and stay there. I don't mean to be accusatory, but odds are the saboteur is a member of the crew. If they've planted anything on board after we took off, I'll find it."

"Oh God," Melina whispered. "Is it that serious?"

"It's the President, ma'am. Everything is serious."

He left the cockpit then and instructed Trent to stay by the door. He found the relief crew laughing and chatting with Merrill outside of the galley. Merrill played along with the crew, but his eyes were shrewd, and he crossed his arms in a way that kept his right hand close to his weapon. Merrill, like most of the agents here, had been present for the recent attacks on the President. He had learned the hard way to always remain sharp.

Jake caught his eye, and Merrill nodded. The playful smile vanished, replaced by a stony, professional look.

Dana and Franz noticed the change and looked at Jake, their own smiles fading. Franz's eyes narrowed, briefly, but long enough for Jake to pick up on it.

"Is everything okay?" Dana asked.

"We're working through the communications problem," Jake replied. "For the moment, I'm asking for the crew to remain seated in the relief cabin."

"You mean us two," Franz said, a slight irritation in his voice. "I assume Captain Sontag and First Officer Vox will remain in the cockpit to operate the aircraft?"

Jake met Franz's eyes. "I am not in the mood for attitude, Mr. Wagner, nor am I in the mood for jokes. You are crew aboard Air Force One, and when you are given an instruction by a Secret Service agent, you will follow it without question and without hesitation. Are we clear?"

Franz's eyes narrowed again. It could just be wounded pride, but Jake decided he would have Franz watched, just in case. "Crystal, Special Agent."

"Outstanding," Jake said. "Special Agent Merrill will escort you to the relief cabin and remain there until further notice."

Merrill nodded acknowledgment and gestured toward the front of the plane. "This way, please."

Jake tapped his earpiece, then remembered that onboard radios were down. He sighed and made his way to the main cabin, where Jess was working at her laptop. The bleak look on her face did little to encourage him.

"Well, I'll say one thing," she told Jake. "Air Force One has a badass electronics suite. This is the first time in my career I've been unable to counter electronic interference."

"Not unable," Jake said, "that's not an option. This is the first time you've been delayed. *Briefly* delayed. Understood?"

Jess's lips tightened slightly. She wasn't used to Jake speaking to her like this. "Sir, yes sir," she said, playfully, but not really. "If you'll permit this agent to make a suggestion, sir, this agent would—"

"Come off it, Jess. I'm not in the mood."

"What else is new? I was only going to say that rather than trying to bludgeon or pry my way through the interference, I could backtrack through the plane's digital logs and determine the source of the interruption. Then, I might be able to cut out the interference altogether. I think that's a better bet than trying to force my way through."

"Good idea. Get on it."

"Wow. Really? Do you actually think I have a good idea? Well, first thing I'm doing when I get through to the outside world is buying a lottery ticket."

Jake rolled his eyes. "Thank you, Jess."

"Sir, yes, sir."

Jake sighed and headed for the President's stateroom. Jess liked to cope with stress by making jokes and being silly. It didn't mean that she wasn't taking her job seriously or that she wasn't putting her full attention into her work, but it grated on Jake. In his mind, work was work and fun was fun, and while he appreciated friendly banter among agents, when things were serious, he preferred when Agents were more like Trent and Merrill: serious, professional and devoid of humor.

The fact that he was dwelling on this so much only showed his own stress. He took a deep breath and released it slowly before reaching the stateroom. It wouldn't do for the President or his family to see him anxious, and Sheila, at least, would see through his gruff façade to the worry behind it.

Coulson nodded at Jake when Jake reached the stateroom. For a younger agent, he was doing an outstanding job of maintaining his own professional demeanor. "Head to the main cabin," Jake told him. "You're assigned to shadow Jess while she tries to reopen communications."

Coulson nodded and moved off. Jake knocked on the door, and as protocol required, Special Agent Patel called, "Identify yourself."

"It's Mercer," Jake said.

Jake waited patiently as Patel checked the hidden camera feed just inside the door to verify Jake's identity. A moment later, the door opened, and Patel—gun drawn—visually identified Jake. He nodded and holstered his weapon, then asked, "What is it, sir?"

"I'm moving you to watch the door. Roberts and Gutierrez will remain in the room. Coulson is shadowing Jess, and Trent and Merrill are watching the crew." Jake thought a moment, then said, "Actually, I want Gutierrez at the galley. I can't imagine Chef Trumbull's turned traitor, but we should cover all of our bases."

"Agreed, sir. Gutierrez!"

Gutierrez left his post at the President's couch and approached the two senior agents. "Sirs?"

"You're to watch the galley and the chef's quarters next door," Jake said. "Chef Trumbull is expected to remain in one of those two rooms for the time being."

"Understood, sir."

Gutierrez left to take his post, and Jake walked into the stateroom. The President sat on one end of the couch, his wife on the other. Both of them glared at Jake, Carrie somewhat more hatefully than Bryan.

Sheila sat in between them, her shoulders bunched with tension, her eyes puffy. She wasn't crying now, but Jake could tell she had earlier. She looked at Jake hopefully, desperate to hear good news from him. He wished that he had some.

Roberts stood in the corner of the room, unobtrusive and present at the same time, like a good agent. Jake nodded at him briefly before addressing the President.

"Mr. President," he said, "At this time, we are investigating an interruption in our internal and external communications. I regret to inform you that we have some evidence that this event may have been caused by sabotage."

"Oh, Jesus," Carrie interrupted. "Are you serious? How does this happen?"

"That's what my team and I are working on right now, ma'am."

"Well, that's nice to hear, but meanwhile we're once more in danger because you can't seem to do your job right."

"Mom!" Sheila cried. "Stop it!"

"No! I'm not going to stop it! This whole thing he has with you is inappropriate in the extreme, and it's clearly keeping him from protecting you properly. I'm tired of turning a blind eye just because he used to be your father's friend."

"Carrie," Bryan said, softly but with the same air of quiet command that had won him the Presidency. "That's enough for now."

Carrie shot a glance at her husband that was so venomous, Jake might have had probable cause to consider her a threat to his life. Her lips trembled, and after a moment, she got to her feet and stormed into the private bedroom. She tried to slam the door, but the dampener's allowed only a gentle whisper, which no doubt worsened her attitude.

Bryan frowned at Jake, his eyes only slightly less venomous than his wife's.

Wonderful, Jake thought. *Now, I'm going to get blamed for Carrie's misdirected fear.* Aloud, he said, "Rest assured we are taking every possible precaution to ensure yours and your family's safety. For now, that means we would like the three of you to remain in this cabin."

"I can't be with you?" Sheila blurted out.

Jake shook his head. "No, ma'am. It's easier for us to keep you all safe if you stay here."

"So you have no idea what's going on," Bryan asked.

Jake debated telling him about the message they'd intercepted in the cockpit but decided against it. The family was already on the verge of panic. "We're looking into things right now."

Bryan sighed and shook his head. "All right. Well, if that's all, then I'd like to go to bed. It's getting late."

Jake took the thinly veiled hint. "Of course, sir."

He nodded and left, feeling Sheila's imploring eyes on him as he walked from the stateroom.

The First Lady's hatred of him combined with Bryan's irritability grated on Jake, but he had bigger things to worry about right now.

Why would someone kill Air Force One's comms but order them to stay on course? Were they trying to lure them out to the open ocean so they could claim it was an accident or systems failure? If that was the case, then why wait? They could just say it happened now. And if they wanted Air Force One to reach Hawaii, then why jam them in the first place?

This event raised more questions than it answered. Jake hated that. He didn't know who their enemy was or what their intentions were. He only knew that they somehow managed to fry the systems of the most secure aircraft on Earth.

How much more dangerous could they be?

CHAPTER FIVE

Night fell quickly and deeply. At forty-five thousand feet, there was no light pollution, and Air Force One's navigational lights barely illuminated the plane itself. The new moon meant that the tapestry of stars—brighter and more numerous than possible anywhere on the ground—were breathtaking.

But to Jake, they were ominous, hard points of light like flashes from rifle fire. He sighed and continued his patrol. With the appropriate parts of the aircraft under guard and Jess working diligently on the communications block, there was little for him to do but patrol and monitor the situation.

And think.

The message the cockpit received was unusual. It didn't read like a threat. It read more like an exhortation. *The President must proceed to Hawaii.*

Why? What was happening in Hawaii? The President was on vacation. He was going incognito. If the goal was to kill him, then Air Force One would be a better place to accomplish that. It was a far more spectacular, public, and terrifying way to kill him than to kill him while he was surfing and snorkeling with his family. And if the goal was to get him to Hawaii, jamming their communications and cutting them off from satellite navigation was the absolute opposite of what they needed to do.

He looked out the window at the dark sky. Something was off. Something didn't make sense. Something outside of the plane.

It hit him like a bolt of lightning. Air Force. Where were their Air Force escorts? With no communications for nearly two hours, and the plane crossing into the open waters of the Pacific, the Air Force should have scrambled jets to intercept and figure out what was going on? Where were they?

Someone must have replaced Air Force One's signal with a duplicate. That was the only explanation. Air Force One was still on course to Hawaii, and someone was communicating with the Air Force as though they were Air Force One.

Now, it made sense. The saboteurs wanted Air Force One to stay on course because that prevented anyone from becoming suspicious. Dammit, they had almost duped them out into open waters.

Jake immediately headed for the cockpit to tell the pilot to turn around. It would be Dana Porter now, but Jake would wake Captain Sontag and give him the instruction too so both pilots were aware of the new plan.

He opened the door that separated the main cabin from the hallway that led to the President's stateroom and the cockpit and saw a man holding Patel from behind and injecting something into his neck. Patel's wide eyes met Jake's, then rolled into the back of his head as the sedative took effect.

Instantly, Jake sprung into action, throwing himself at the terrorist. He couldn't identify the man at first, but after dodging a swipe with the needle and driving his fist into the attacker's stomach, he saw the grimacing face of Franz Wagner.

It was sabotage, after all.

Franz swiped with the needle again, but Jake had caught him off guard. He easily blocked the strike and headbutted Wagner in the nose. Wagner cried out and flinched backwards, giving Jake an opening to his groin.

Jake took advantage of that opening. The moment his knee collided with Wagner's groin, the copilot jumped into the air and fell to the ground, gasping and clutching his wounded member.

Jake drew his weapon and said, "Move and you die."

Franz glared up at Jake, but it was clear he wasn't going to be able to move for a while. He heard footsteps pounding and looked up to see Gutierrez rushing his way. The agent's weapon was drawn, and his face was tense with fear.

"Sir, Trent and Merrill are down. They're alive, but they're unconscious."

"The crew?"

"Captain Sontag and First Officer Vox are sleeping. They don't appear to be injured."

"Go wake them up now. I want them in the cockpit, and I want Dana Porter in the relief cabin under guard."

"Yes, sir."

Jake reached up to knock on the President's door, but it opened before he could, and his fist clinked against the barrel of Roberts' gun. Roberts quickly covered Franz, who had uncurled from his fetal position but wisely chose to remain on the ground. "I heard the noise, sir. Oh God, is Patel down?"

"Temporarily," Jake said. "Wagner injected him, Trent and Merrill with a sedative."

"Jake?" Sheila's voice called from inside the stateroom. "Is that you?"

"Stay inside!" Jake called. "Roberts, keep the door closed and locked and stay with the President's family."

"Yes, sir."

Roberts did as he was told, and a moment later, Gutierrez came back, "Sontag and Vox are in the cockpit. They've elected to divert to the nearest airfield."

"No!" Wagner cried. He tried to sit up, but Jake planted his boot on Wagner's chest and slammed him back to the ground.

"Good," Jake said. Then he frowned. "Where's Dana Porter?"

"Trent's awake. He has her under guard."

"All right. Help me with him."

Jake and Gutierrez quickly bound Wagner's wrists and ankles together and carried him back to the relief cabin. Trent appeared groggy, but his grip on his weapon was firm. Merrill sat in the other relief chair, his head between his knees.

"Do you need medical?" Jake asked. "Either of you?"

Trent shook his head. Merrill looked up and said, "I feel all right at the moment. Thank you, Jake. Give me five minutes, and I'll be ready to work."

"Make it ten. I need everyone sharp. Gutierrez?"

"Sir."

"Search their belongings. All four of them. Actually, search everyone's belongings."

He heard the pounding of feet behind him and turned to see Coulson and Jess, weapons drawn. Coulson nodded at Jake. "I heard, sir. Shall I assist Gutierrez?"

"Do it. Merrill, I'm going to stay here with you and talk to our relief crew. You'll resume guard duties. Gutierrez, before you leave, handcuff Dana to the chair."

"No!" Dana cried, flinching away from the agent. Jake trained his weapon on her and said, "Any more resistance from you, and I'll take care of that permanently."

"You can't fire a gun in here!" Dana protested. "If you punch a hole in the hull—"

"These are .22s," Jake said. "Not enough power to punch through the hull or the windows, but more than enough power to shred your brain."

Dana paled another shade and began to tremble. "Please. I didn't know anything about this."

She tensed when Gutierrez grabbed her wrist, but when Jake's eyes narrowed, she allowed herself to be handcuffed.

"That true, Wagner?" Jake asked, keeping his eyes on Dana.

"Fuck you."

Well, Jake didn't expect it to be easy.

"So you were fine with your copilot disappearing and making a commotion outside of the cockpit while flying the President over open waters at night?"

"He said he had to use the bathroom."

"You have a bathroom in the cockpit."

"The one in the cabin is bigger."

Jake nodded and holstered his weapon. The plane began to bank, and Jake watched Dana's eyes widen and shift toward the cockpit. It wasn't a surefire sign of guilt, but then, neither was Franz's attitude earlier.

"We're diverting to the nearest airfield," Jake informed them. There's been an attack on the President, and we suspect the two of you are involved."

"I didn't know anything! I promise you!"

"Your word doesn't mean anything when the President's life was threatened. I don't mean to be an asshole, but I don't particularly care if that's what I am right now."

Merrill stood and drew his weapon. "I'm good to go, sir."

If it were any other agent, Jake would have asked him if he was sure, but Merrill was one of the finest men under Jake's supervision. If he said he was good, it was because he was certain he could protect the President.

"Good. Go check on Patel."

Merrill nodded and headed down the cabin. Jake reached down and hefted Wagner onto the relief chair Merrill had vacated. The crewman glared at Jake and spat, "You're all going to die."

Dana paled slightly at that and began to tremble. Franz noticed it and turned his glare to her.

Jake turned to Dana and squatted down right in front of her. "Anything you want to tell me, Dana?"

“Fuck you!” Franz shouted. “You and all of the imperialists will—”

Jake backhanded him hard across the face. He fell to the deck, crying out in pain and anger. Jake reached into one of his belt pockets and pulled out a small roll of duct tape. He grinned at Franz. "Can't go wrong with a classic."

“Fuck—”

The rest of it was cut off when Jake pressed a strip of the adhesive tape tightly against Franz’s mouth. He lifted the terrorist back onto his chair and turned back to Dana.

“Time to talk,” he said. “Unless you want the same treatment.” Dana’s eyes flew to him, and her face paled. “I don’t care if you’re a woman,” Jake said. “That will earn you exactly zero favors. Start telling me what I want to know, or I’ll make it hurt. Badly.”

Dana glanced at Franz, and Jake nodded. He reached forward and started to uncuff Dana.

“No!” she protested. “I didn’t know anything! I promise you! Please!”

Jake finished uncuffing Dana wordlessly.

“Please!” She cried out, “Please don’t!”

When her hands were free, Jake grabbed her right armpit and hauled her to her feet. She stumbled and struggled to pull away, but Jake kept her upright.

“No!” she shouted. “Please! I’m begging you, I didn’t know who he was!”

Jake fought back a wave of self-revulsion. He didn’t feel guilty doing what he needed to do to determine the nature of the threat against the President, but if Dana really was incident, he would feel terrible about this.

But the President came first. Sheila came first.

“Last chance to be honest with me, Dana,” Jake said. “Tell me what’s going on.”

“Please…” she whispered.

She didn’t finish. A loud thud shook the plane, and Jake was thrown off of his feet, sprawling on top of his captive.

He instantly regained his feet and grabbed Dana. “What the hell was that?”

“I don’t know,” the woman repeated.

But there was a flash of triumph in her eyes that told Jake all he needed to know. He glared at her and spun her around. She didn’t resist as he handcuffed her, and she kept that odd look of triumph on her face when Jake sat her across from Franz. Franz laughed with glee and stared mockingly at Jake. The cockpit door opened just as Jake cuffed Dana back into her seat, and Trent exited. His face was etched with fear. “Sir, the right outboard engine just exploded.”

Jake's blood froze. He heard soft laughter behind him and turned, expecting to see Franz laughing again. Instead, he saw Dana smiling at him. "Checkmate, special agent."

CHAPTER SIX

"Watch these two," Jake instructed Trent.

He walked into the cockpit to see Ian and Melina gripping their yokes with white knuckles and whiter faces.

"What happened?" he asked.

"Engine four just blew up on us," Ian replied, his voice controlled but tense. "We cut off fuel to the engine and fire suppression extinguished the blaze, but the engine is gone and there's damage to the outer flap."

"What does that mean?"

"Well, if we can still touch down at Edwards Air Force Base, not much. We can still fly on three engines, and the damage is localized. Frankly, though, we got lucky. That blast should have torn off half our wing."

"Meaning if there's another, we could fall from the sky."

"Yes."

Jake pursed his lips. "Can you take us lower to the ground?"

"Not yet. There's an insane amount of air traffic over California. With no satellite navigation, we can't see that traffic, and at night, I don't want to rely on visual identification or sonar to avoid a collision."

"So we're stuck here?"

"I'm afraid so, sir. We're hoping the Air Force will figure things out soon and send some jets up to assess the situation, but with no way to talk to them, I have no way of knowing if they'll let us land."

"They'll let us land. The President is on board. As soon as you see Air Force jets, head toward Edwards. The Air Force will figure it out and clear traffic for us. Can you navigate to the runway with no satellite?"

"Yes, sir. I still have lidar and sonar. The air base will have transmitters in those bands to guide us to a safe landing."

"You'd better not do that!" a voice called from outside the cockpit.

Jake frowned and turned to see Trent holding the cockpit door open, his face ashen. The voice came from Dana, who grinned hatefully at Jake and explained. "I told your buddy something you might want to hear. That's why he walked in on your little conversation."

Jake's eyes narrowed. "What is it?"

"That wasn't the only bomb, Special Agent. We have some more waiting to be detonated. If you land this airplane anywhere but where we tell you, all of them will go off at once. I suggest turning around and maintaining our course to Hawaii."

"No," Jake said.

Trent turned his eyes sharply to Jake. Behind Jake, Ian and Melina gasped.

Dana blinked. "What?"

"I don't repeat myself. Captain, proceed in a holding pattern until the Air Force shows up."

"Shall we demonstrate that we're not bluffing?" Dana asked. "I'd be more than happy to prove our sincerity to you."

"You can't program a bomb to detonate upon landing at some locations but not others."

"Perhaps not. Or perhaps it is only the plane's GPS that is hampered."

Jake's eyes narrowed. "You're saying that the bombs can tell where we're headed?"

"I'm saying make your own choices, but know that the choice you're making now will result in the destruction of Air Force One."

Jake glared at Dana. His hands curled into fists. He wanted to tell her to go screw herself and tell Trent to shut the door.

But he couldn't. Dana could be bluffing, but the consequences if she wasn't were beyond catastrophic.

He nodded and kept his eyes on the terrorist as he said, "Captain Sontag, can we make Hawaii on three engines?"

"Yes. It will take us longer, and we'll have to descend and use a modified course to avoid airline traffic, but we can make it."

"Is that okay with you, Dana?"

"Perfectly fine. As long as the President reaches Hawaii."

Jake nodded and motioned for Trent to shut the door. He turned around to see Melina crying softly. He wished he could think of something to say to comfort her, but there really wasn't anything to say. Air Force One had been hijacked by terrorists, and right now, those terrorists had the upper hand.

Jake turned to the captain. "How long can we fly before we need to refuel?"

"Ten hours," the captain said. "I can stretch it to twelve if I reduce speed, but that's the most I can give you."

"Can you make it take twelve hours to reach Hawaii?"

"Sure, I could do that."

"Do it. Buy us as much time as you can."

"I will. Please be careful, sir."

Jake's safety wasn't remotely important right now, but he didn't argue the point. He returned to the relief cabin and shut the door. Dana and Franz grinned mockingly at him.

It occurred to Jake that neither of them had thought to barter for their freedom. He found that odd. He wasn't sure if it meant they were bluffing or if it meant that they felt in control of the situation, whether they were bound or not.

"Trent, tear the tape off of Franz's mouth."

Trent obliged, yanking the duct tape off without even a semblance of gentleness. Franz swore and glared at Trent, blood welling around his lips where the tape had torn his facial hair out.

"Why did you poison my agents?" Jake asked. "Why were you trying to get into the President's stateroom?"

Franz spat on him. "Go to hell, bastard."

Jake ignored the surge of rage that coursed through him and wiped the spittle off. "I'm only asking because if you have bombs on the plane, it seems to me like the easiest thing to do would be to just blow us up."

Trent cast shocked eyes to his boss. "Sir—"

Jake held a hand up. "Can you explain that to me?" he asked Franz.

Franz chuckled. "We will kill everyone on board, make no mistake. All good things in time."

"In Hawaii, you mean," Jake said. "Why Hawaii?"

"Why not?" Franz mocked. "It is beautiful there. What better place to die?"

"Is there a reason Bard wants the President killed in Hawaii?"

"Who is Bard?" Franz asked.

"Trident. Is there a reason Trident wants—"

He stopped when Franz threw his head back and laughed. "Wow," the terrorist said. "You really know nothing."

"So what's the goal then? What's the point? Trident's tried to kill the President before. Why is Hawaii so important?"

"You keep saying Trident," Dana interrupted. "You keep trying to trip us up by shocking us with all of this knowledge you think you have. Consider, perhaps, that maybe you don't know nearly as much as you think you do."

"So help me understand. You could just blow us up, but you choose not to?"

"Do you not have failsafes for your plans? We don't want to blow you up. We want you to go to Hawaii. If you refuse, the destruction of this airplane and everyone on board is our failsafe. That is all you need to know, and all we're going to tell you."

Jake met Dana's eyes. The woman kept a defiant and contemptuous glare as she held Jake's gaze. After a moment, Jake said, "Make sure both of them are bound tightly to their chairs, Trent. You can leave the gags off for now. Maybe they'll get an urge to talk."

"Don't count on it, asshole," Franz said.

He spat again, but Jake sidestepped, and the phlegm landed in his partner's lap instead. Dana recoiled in disgust, and Franz paled a little. "Sorry."

So Dana was in charge. That was something Jake could work with.

He headed toward the main cabin, but the door to the President's stateroom flew open, and the First Lady stormed for him. Special Agent Roberts grabbed her shoulder and called, "Ma'am. You have to stay in—"

Carrie whirled on Roberts and shrieked. "Put your hands on me again, and I'll have you arrested!"

Roberts looked at Jake, and Jake lifted his hand. Roberts released Carrie and retreated. When Carrie realized that Roberts had asked Jake's permission before agreeing to release her, she turned a mottled shade of purple.

"You asshole!" she screamed at Jake. "*You* are not in *charge* here!"

"I'm sorry, ma'am," Jake said, keeping his cool, "But I am."

"No! You are a *bodyguard!* A *servant!* How dare you—"

"Mom!" Sheila called, poking her head out of the door. "Stop it! Let them do their jobs!"

"Oh, what, so the terrorists can blow us up? Yeah, great job, Jake. You're so deep inside Sheila you've convinced her you can do no wrong, even when a fucking *bomb* goes off—"

"Carrie."

Once more, the President spoke with that calm voice of authority. This time, Carrie resisted. "No, Bryan! Dammit, this is your *family!* This has nothing to do with the goddamned country. Your *family* is in danger. Your *daughter* is in danger. Will you both stop treating Jake like a god and take charge of the situation?"

"I am," Bryan replied. "I'm choosing to allow the Secret Service to do its job and handle this situation. We're not trained. They are. Get back in the room and stay out of their way."

"Stay out…" Carrie clenched her hands into fists and shook visibly. She turned to Jake, her eyes sick with hate. "I wish to God you would just die.."

"Mom!" Sheila shouted. "Stop it! Get in the room!"

Carrie stalked into the room, shoving past her husband and daughter. Sheila met Jake's eyes, guilt, fear and worry all playing in her expression.

Bryan met Jake's eyes as well, and though it was unwarranted, the soft accusation in the President's gaze cut Jake to his core.

The door slid shut, and Jake sighed and continued his journey to the main cabin. Coulson and Gutierrez arrived at the same time. Both agents were frowning.

"We couldn't find anything, sir. We checked everyone's bags, even yours and Jess's. There's nothing."

Jake sighed and shook his head. "All right. Return to your posts for now. Actually, better idea. Gutierrez, go back to your post. Coulson, I want you with the President. You'll assist Roberts until further notice."

The two agents nodded acknowledgment and headed toward the front of the plane. Jake sighed and walked over to Jess. "Anything helpful?"

"Depends on what you mean by helpful."

Jake rubbed the bridge of his nose. He didn't have the energy for wordplay. "Just tell me what you have, Jess."

"I have evidence that there was a ground-based component to the loss of communications."

He lifted his eyes. "Really? What component?"

"Just before we lost radio and satellite, the onboard computers suffered a massive power surge. That surge originated from outside of the plane."

"Where on the ground?"

"I don't know. The log ends there."

"Keep working on getting past the jamming frequency. And let's hope the Navy and Air Force wonder why we're flying lower, slower and more meanderingly. It would be really nice to see a friendly face in these skies right now.

Even if there's no much they can do.

CHAPTER SEVEN

"It's an inside job," Jake said. "It has to be."

Jess frowned at him. "Well, yeah. You already confirmed that two of the crew are involved."

"No, not that," Jake said. "I mean the ground attack. The EM pulse that was fired on Air Force One concurrent with the system shorting out."

The two of them were sitting together in the main cabin. It was an hour after Jake had interrogated the relief crew, eleven hours until they were forced to land or run out of fuel. Jake had spent that hour touching base with the cockpit crew and with each of his agents to ensure that expectations were set and that he was kept aware of every piece of information. So far, nothing has changed. After their taunting session, Dana and Franz had clammed up, only saying that Air Force One had better remain on its course to Hawaii. Ian and Melina appeared in somewhat better shape. Melina was no longer weeping, and Ian seemed far more relaxed now that they had a plan of action.

The agents as well were in control of themselves. Trent clearly wished the terrorists would give him an excuse to act violently, but he retained his professional calm. Patel had medical training, and he confirmed that the sedatives Franz had given the three of them were nontoxic.

That only raised another question: why sedate them? Why not kill them? Not that Jake was ungrateful, it just made no sense. What was their endgame here? Why was Hawaii so important?

There was no way to answer that question and no way to rescue the President without restoring communications, however, so that was Jake's number one priority. He and Jess were touching base to determine how they could do that.

"You think our mole had something to do with it?"

"I think that would be, what, the fifth confirmed mole?"

"Only the second confirmed one," Jess said. "The juries out on the other two, and there's no fifth I'm aware of."

Since Trident's campaign against the President, there had been rumors of a mole within the Secret Service who was feeding information to the terrorist group. Those rumors had been confirmed when Commander Dalton—the commanding officer of the Secret Service's Rapid Response Teams—had been caught red-handed conspiring with Eli Bard. Dalton was still at large, as was Bard. Both had slipped capture and remained thorns in Jake's side.

But suspicion remained on at least two other secret service agents. It was possible, in fact, that one of them had engineered the attack, and there was no fifth or even fourth mole.

Not that it made things all that much better.

"Well, if it's not Secret Service, the only other thing I could think of is another disgruntled former military member."

"You think your old friend Drew might have recruited someone?"

"I think we're reaching," Jake said, shaking his head. "Let's focus on what we know. We know that an external attack caused or at least exacerbated the loss of communications. We know that whatever caused that loss also prevented the Air Force from realizing that we're in distress."

"Not to be pedantic," Jess interrupted, "but those two events could have different causes. Disrupting our communications and creating false communications would have to be propagated by two different machines, unless Bard is once again using some bleeding edge tech that I don't know about."

"Let's not rule that out," Jake replied.

In their last conflict with Trident, an international arms dealer known as Hadad had stolen sensitive data from a secret weapons research facility. If Bard still had any amount of that information, then he could have equipment beyond the state of the art. Jake could only hope that wasn't the case, but hope didn't solve mysteries, evidence did.

And right now, they had precious little evidence.

"Is there a way we can establish some sort of internal communication?" Jake asked. "I'm going to look through the plane for signs of anything out of the ordinary."

"Again?"

"Yes, again. But this time, with your eyes."

"You don't just want me to look?"

"No, I want you to keep trying to determine the source of the EM pulse, keep trying to restore communications and also help me find anything out of the ordinary on the aircraft."

"Gee, is that all?" Jess asked drily.

"You can do it," he said.

"Great pep talk, boss."

"It's not a pep talk. It's both a recognition of your talents and an instruction. Sorry if I'm being intense, but—"

"Intense? You? No way."

Jake was surprised to feel himself crack a smile. "Jess, I really need you to help me here. You're my tech girl. You can see things I can't."

Jess sighed. "Let me fiddle with some things. Finding a signal we can use isn't the issue, but finding a way to cobble together two transceivers with the portable equipment we have is challenging. Give me a few minutes to put something together."

"Thank you."

He left Jess to work and headed toward the President's cabin in the meantime. He wasn't sure if it was a good idea to inform the President of their progress, but the only real risk was the First Lady panicking, and Bryan seemed to have that under control. Maybe letting him know that they had a lead would help calm them.

Don't make excuses, he thought. *You just want to see Sheila.*

He felt a pang of guilt. He really was just making up a reason to assure her that everything would be all right.

But they did have the situation under control, at least for the moment, and his news really was good.

Not yet, it's not. Not until you reestablish communication.

He pushed his worries aside and knocked on the stateroom door, nodding at Patel, who stood guard outside the room.

"Identify yourself," Coulson called from inside.

"It's Mercer," Jake said.

"Confirmed," Patel called.

The door slid open, revealing both Coulson and Roberts with their weapons drawn. "Good job, boys," Jake said, "Mr. President, may I speak with you?"

Bryan stood in the center of the room, his hands clasped behind his back, a scowl on his face. That was a sign that he was frustrated with being unable to do anything about their circumstances. Jake understood the feeling. "What is it, Jake?" he asked irritably.

"Sir, we've determined that the loss of communications was due in part to an EM attack from the ground. We're currently working on ways to restore communications and alert the Air Force of our predicament."

"And that's supposed to make me feel better?"

Jake blinked. "Well… we're closer to finding an answer—"

"Tell me, Jake. When the next bomb goes off, what's the difference between being an inch from safety and being a mile from safety?"

"I'm not sure sir."

"Nothing. Not a goddamned thing. Jake, I know you're working your ass off out there, but do me a favor, don't come back until you have good news. I can't deal with Carrie having another meltdown right now."

Jake nodded and looked around the cabin.

"She's in the bedroom with her mother," Bryan said, correctly guessing who Jake was looking for. "Leave her there."

"Yes, sir," Jake said softly. "I'll get us out of this, Bryan. I always have."

The tension in Bryan's eyes softened just slightly. "I know you'll do your best, Jake."

Jake left the stateroom and headed back to Jess. When he arrived, Jess said, "I take it from your scowl that things didn't go well?"

"Well, the First Lady didn't tear me limb from limb, so it could have been worse."

"Ouch. That bad, huh?"

"Yep. I'm hoping you can cheer me up."

Jess grinned. "I might have just the ticket."

She handed Jake what looked like a sculpture of a headset constructed from paper clips and duct tape. "This is an ultra-low-frequency transceiver. It's the first of its kind that I'm aware of. Are you familiar with the concept of infrasound?"

"Not at all."

"Well, I don't feel like teaching right now, so I'll keep it short. We can use these"—she held up another one—"to talk, and as a bonus, our communication will be undetectable. It's ridiculously short range, but it should work for something the size of this aircraft. It won't give me high-resolution images, but it'll give me something to look at."

"Outstanding. Thank you."

"Of course." She set one of the transceivers on her head. "I would suggest checking the crew lockers again. If something on board is influencing communication at all, it's almost certainly in the crew's luggage. Everything else was looked at by a thousand different eyes."

"And yet they still missed the bomb in the engine and possibly bombs elsewhere on the craft."

"No one's perfect. Besides, I just said start there, I didn't say finish there."

"Fair enough."

Jake left the cabin and headed for the crew lockers. The lockers were ahead of the galley before the cabin restroom, where Jake had been interrogating Sheila when the bomb went off. Gutierrez and Coulson had already searched them, but Jake had expert help now. He opened Franz's locker first and said, "Jess, can you hear me?"

"Yeah, I hear you."

The connection sounded murky, like they were underwater, but Jake could understand her. "Can you see inside the locker?"

"It kind of looks like those old video games where you had to invade a high school run by a telepathic student."

"What?"

"Yeah, she was a government experiment with psychic superpowers who… never mind. I can see. What's that in the corner?"

"This?" Jake picked up a black plastic brick about twice the size of a deck of cards. "It looks like an old cassette player."

"Open it up." Jake pressed the eject button, and Jess said, "From the back."

Jake turned it over and said, "How?"

"Seriously? Jake, come on. You have a multitool, right? Use the screwdriver and open the box."

Jake felt heat climb his cheeks as he retrieved his multitool. "You don't need to be a brat about it."

"Come on, Jake. You're staring at two screws, and you're asking me how to open it."

"All right, I get it."

Jake unscrewed both sides of the back housing of the box and carefully removed it. The jumble of wires inside meant nothing to him, but apparently they meant something to Jess.

"Bingo. Look behind the three large wires looped around the left-center of the box."

Jake did that and said, "There's a little vial of silver fluid with two little bumps on the end."

"Yep. That, my friend, is a low-powered electronic pulse emitter."

"Electronic… *this* is the jammer?"

"No. This contains barely enough power to operate a watch. *But*, if our radios are already compromised, then that little number can release enough noise to keep the system from rebooting. Pull it out of the machine and crush it with your boot."

Jake did that, and said, "Is that mercury?"

"Yes, but it's not unless you drink it. By the way, the plane's communications software is rebooting."

Jake's eyes widened. "We have radio?"

"Radio and navigation. And you can say it now. Who's awesome?"

Jake grinned. "You're awesome."

"Damned right."

CHAPTER EIGHT

“Air Force One, say again. You are *where?”*

"Check your GPS," Jake told the Air Force lieutenant colonel on the other end of the radio. "We are in the North Pacific at the following coordinates."

He read the coordinates off to the colonel, and when he finished, the woman said, “That puts you… Jesus, that’s over five hundred miles off course. And… I’m sorry, can you identify yourself again?”

Jake sighed. “This is Special Agent Jake Mercer of the Secret Service. Air Force One has been sabotaged by terrorists. We are currently proceeding in a slow and meandering fashion toward Honolulu, Hawaii. Our engine… what number did you say, Captain?”

“Engine number four.”

“Engine number four was destroyed by an explosion caused by a bomb planted by said terrorists. We were told by the terrorists that more bombs are onboard the plane, and if we don’t land in Hawaii, those bombs will go off.”

There was a brief pause, then the colonel said, “All right, sir. This is a secure line. We do *not* have time for prank calls. Call this number again, and you will be reported to the FBI.”

“Dammit, colonel, if you don’t believe me, look us up! I know you can see us. We’ve been shouting at your radar for the past five hours!”

“That was you? I mean… Sir, we’ve been communicating with Air Force One the whole…”

She stopped again, clearly unsure how much to say.

Jake sighed. “Captain, how close are we to the nearest military base?”

“That would probably be Lewis-McChord,” the captain replied, “but Eielson might reach us faster.”

“Did you hear that, colonel? Scramble some jets and see for yourself. The Air Force One you’re communicating with is not the real Air Force One. We’re the real Air Force One, and we’re in trouble.”

The colonel remained silent. Jake waited a long moment, then said, “Colonel, if I’m lying to you, then you chose to investigate a threat of a bomb that will destroy Air Force One and kill the President only to find out it was a prank call. Would you rather get chewed out for wasting a couple hours of AWACS time, or would you rather be the colonel who ignored a threat to the President and watch him get blown up a few hours from now?"

The silence on the other end was long enough that Jake feared the colonel had hung up on them. Finally, though, he heard her say, "We'll call NORAD. They might be able to get a satellite image faster than we can send a reconnaissance mission."

"Thank you," Jake said.

He turned to the captain and said, "Can we still make Hawaii if we keep heading north for another few minutes before turning South?"

"We can, but we're going to have to be more direct. It's going to shave two hours off of our flight time."

"That's fine. Hopefully we can get this resolved in a way so it won't matter. Can you call Hawaii?"

"I can try satellite communications with Midway. That's the only thing that will reach right now."

"Do it. I want them to be looking for any threats that we might face when we land. These guys have a real strong desire for us to make Hawaii, and I want whatever they have in store dealt with."

"Should we tell them we have systems back?" Melina asked.

Jake shook his head. "No. We have the upper hand right now. We can keep this card close to our chest for the time being. I want to wait until we have the situation under control on the ground before we reveal everything."

"You don't think that they'll be afraid of the fighter escorts?"

Jake regarded Melina. She was young for a first officer on a jumbo jet, even if she were a civilian pilot. Her file indicated that she was the youngest member of the White House Military Office. Technically speaking, she was an Air Force lieutenant colonel, but in practice, the Military Office rarely used military ranks. Normally, that would put her in her late thirties or early forties, but she appeared to be in her late twenties.

She was every bit as naïve as her age suggested. "No," Jake told her. "They had to have anticipated this possibility. They'll try to find another way to win. They can't do much tied up as they are, but since we don't need to reveal anything right now, we won't. I don't want them to have the slightest chance of adjusting to this information."

Melina nodded. "I understand."

Jake doubted that, but her compliance was more important than her understanding.

The radio buzzed again. It was the Air Force.

"All right," the officer from before said, her voice tense. "I believe you. You're where you say you are, and you're who you say you are. What do you need from us?"

Jake looked at Ian. "Can you reach Hawaii?"

"No. No one's answering, anyway."

"Then that's what I need from you, Colonel. The terrorists insist that the President must land in Hawaii, and they've warned us of a GPS-based detonator that will ignite more bombs if the wheels touch down anywhere other than Honolulu. I don't know what they have planned for us when we land, but I'd very much like for there to be a large military and law enforcement presence as soon as we touch down. I want the President and his family in protective custody the moment they walk off the plane."

"Understood, sir. My superiors have directed me to send you a fighter escort as well as a refueling tanker. Please turn east. The fighters will be coming from Yokota Air Force Base. They should rendezvous with you in one hour. The tanker will reach you an hour after that. Once you and the fighters have refueled, you can proceed south to Hawaii again. We'll have another tanker en route to replenish the fighters."

"Can we make it that far on three engines?" Jake asked the captain.

"We can, but if we lose another engine, we're done for."

"We'll have to hope that doesn't happen. All right, colonel, we're proceeding east. Let's get this done."

He cut off the channel and told the Captain, I'm going to update the President, but call me if you need anything, or if anything happens that I should know."

"Will do. Thank you, sir."

"Same goes for you, First Officer Vox."

Melina gave him a distracted half-smile, and he added, "Chin up, Vox. We're almost out of the woods."

Vox managed a distracted full smile, and Jake decided that was the best he was going to get. He left the cockpit and stopped in the relief cabin on his way to the President's stateroom. Franz and Dana had bloodshot, heavy-lidded eyes, indicating their exhaustion.

"Any chance you want to tell me anything else?" he asked. "I'm feeling generous. I might trade life in prison instead of the death penalty for something that could help resolve this flight non-violently."

Jake didn't have the authority to make that deal, but lying to people trying to kill the President was perfectly fine.

"It doesn't matter," Dana said. "You might have radio back, but you won't succeed. It's a pity. This would have gone much more smoothly if you had just gone to Honolulu as ordered."

Jake glanced at Trent. "I had the door closed, sir. I don't know how they heard."

"I could tell by the smiles on your faces. You think you have us beat, and the only reason for that would be if you have been in contact with your government."

"Well, Jake said, "I'm sure sorry to inconvenience you."

"It doesn't matter. Your mocking doesn't matter. We will prevail."

"Whatever you need to tell yourself."

He left them and headed for the President's stateroom. Rather than knock on the door, he radioed Roberts and Coulson. "Boys, this is Mercer. I'm outside of the door. I have good news for the President."

"Yes, sir," Roberts replied.

He opened the door, and the President looked in surprise between Roberts and Jake. "You have radio back?"

"Radio and navigation," Jake said, "and we've been in contact with the Air Force. They're sending us escorts and a tanker. We're going to make Hawaii after all."

The President grinned. "Outstanding work, Jake. Wait one second, let me call Carrie and Sheila."

He went to the bedroom, and Jake could hear Carrie's raised voice as they argued. Then silence, probably because Bryan was sharing the good news that they had established communication with the Air Force again.

A moment later, the family walked out. Sheila abandoned propriety and rushed into Jake's arms, pressing her lips to his. Jake decided it wasn't worth the effort to try to convince her not to kiss him right then and just kissed her back instead. When she pulled away, she beamed at him and said, "I knew you'd rescue us, Jake."

Jake couldn't resist a smile. "I told you that everything would be okay."

"Sit down, Sheila," Carrie said tersely. "I want to hear what he has to say."

Sheila took a seat on the couch. Her parents elected to stand. The First Lady faced Jake, a frown on her face. Behind the frown, however, Jake could see hope. He took encouragement from that.

“Thanks to the efforts of my partner, Special Agent Foster, we were able to recover the device responsible for disrupting communications and disable it.” That was an oversimplification, but it would do for the purposes of this conversation. “We established contact with the Air Force and received instructions to rendezvous with a fighter escort and a tanker. Once we’ve refueled, we’ll proceed to Hawaii.”

“We’re going on vacation after all?” Sheila asked.

“Well, no,” Jake admitted. “Because of the terrorist attack on board Air Force One, the three of you will be taken into protective custody by the U.S. military at Pearl Harbor. From there, we will arrange for transportation back to the United States.”

“Are we going to take the other Air Force One?” Carrie asked.

Strictly speaking, any fixed-wing aircraft the President was on board became Air Force One, but Carrie was clearly referring to the other Boeing VC-25A. “I’m not sure, ma’am,” Jake admitted. “Most likely not. It’s possible the terrorists sabotaged both planes. I would speculate they’ll prepare a military transport for you. Probably a C-117.”

“What’s a C-117?”

“Doesn’t matter,” Bryan said, cutting off the rabbit trail. “We’re going home. Actually, Jake, I think we'll go to Camp David instead. That way, we can have a little staycation. Or at least my family can."

“I’m sure that can be arranged, sir,” Jake said. “For now, I still want you three to sit tight here in the cabin. I’m sorry your vacation had to start this way, but we’ll make sure that wherever you end up, you get there safely.”

“Thank you, Jake,” Sheila said. “I love you.”

Bryan tensed a little, but quickly repeated, “Thank you, Jake.”

Sheila looked expectantly at her mother. Carrie glared at Jake, but Jake got the impression it was more out of habit than actual anger. “Thank you, Special Agent Mercer.”

That was a start. Jake nodded. “Just doing my duty, ma’am.”

“Do I have to stay here?” Sheila asked. She smiled coyly. “I was thinking you and I—”

“I would prefer you stay here, ma’am,” Jake said quickly. “Just for your security.”

Sheila kept her coy smile and said, “I’ll miss you.”

Carrie’s lips thinned, and the daggers her eyes shot at Jake seemed a lot more genuine now.

Christ, Sheila, could you twist the knife another time?

"I'll pass along updates shortly."

He left the cabin and walked right into Merrill. "Sir, will you proceed to the cabin with me?"

Merrill kept his voice calm, but his eyes communicated his concern. Jake frowned and followed him to the cockpit.

When he arrived, Ian turned to him. "I'm not sure if this is a problem, Jake, but our satellite system is fowled again."

"What? We've lost communication?"

"No, but we've lost navigation. I can still tell from the other flight instruments where we are. The problem is that my readings don't match up with the satellite feed."

"Are you sure it's the satellite that's off and not the analog systems?"

In answer to his question, the radio buzzed. "Air Force One, this is Lieutenant Colonel Frazier. You are nearly a hundred miles off of the course we agreed on. Please advise."

Jake's heart sank.

Well, it's my fault for thinking this would be easy.

CHAPTER NINE

"Colonel Frazier, this is Captain Ian Sontag. I'm adjusting course to return to our agreed-upon route. We're having some trouble with our instruments, but I can use the backups to get back on track."

"In the meantime," Jake interjected, "please keep this line open and monitor our position via satellite. I suspect there is more sabotage occurring. If we deviate again, I want to hear about it."

There was a slight pause on the other end. "I see. Is the President secure?"

"He's secure, but I don't know about the plane."

"Very well. I'll keep an eye on you and remain in communication. Who else is in the cockpit?"

"Captain Sontag, myself, Special Agent Merrill, and... where's First Officer Vox?"

"She's going to the galley to get us some snacks," Ian replied.

Jake frowned. "I'm going to turn you over to Captain Sontag, Colonel." He turned to Merrill. "Next time, Special Agent, call the galley and have Trumbull bring you snacks."

Merrill reddened slightly but maintained his professional demeanor. "Understood. I apologize, sir."

Don't apologize, dammit, Jake didn't say. *Don't make boneheaded mistakes. Christ, Merrill, you know better. That's exactly how Franz sabotaged us.*

Well, lightning didn't strike the same place twice, did it?

Of course it did. Melina wasn't in the galley, and when Jake asked Gutierrez where she was, he frowned and said, "She told me you sent her to ask Jess something. She said there was a glitch in the navigation system.

Dammit. Jake drew his weapon. "With me."

Gutierrez's eyes widened. He drew his weapon and followed Jake. They ran into the main cabin and found Jess on the ground.

"Jess!"

Jake dropped by her side and felt for a pulse. It was strong, but he could see a small welt where a needle had been inserted into her neck.

He checked her laptop. It didn't appear to have been tampered with, but he would need Jess to confirm that.

"Stay with her," he told Gutierrez. "I'm going to find Melina."

He rushed through the cabin. Behind the main cabin was Sheila's personal stateroom, and behind that were quarters that were reserved for the President's entourage, or in this case, the Secret Service agents. Those quarters hadn't been used.

In the very back of the plane was an engineering room with controls for all of the plane's major systems. Jake wasn't surprised to see Melina Vox bent over one of those controls with the cover of an electrical panel removed as she fiddled with the wires underneath.

Jake didn't bother asking her to stop. He rushed forward and tackled her to the ground. She fell with a cry, but almost instantly brought a needle around toward Jake's arm. Jake barely blocked the strike, but it was followed with another, then another.

Timid little Melina Vox was apparently a far better fighter than Franz was. With a twist, she rolled so she was on top of Jake. Using the awkward confines of the room and what appeared to be a solid background in wrestling, she held Jake down and swung the needle low, out of reach of Jake's hand.

Jake had been trained too, though, by the Marine Corps with some help from the Navy SEALs. He shifted his hips and drove his knee into Melina's wrist. The movement redirected the needle toward Melina's own abdomen. With a cry, she released the needle, but in order to avoid the point, she had to weaken the pressure on Jake's chest. Jake rolled over on top of her and applied his own weight to her, smothering her.

She grunted with effort as she struggled, but Jake was significantly larger and stronger than she was, and soon, her efforts waned. Jake waited until she was gasping for breath and no longer struggling, then got quickly to his feet.

He kicked the needle out of the way and dragged her away from the controls. She swiped at the open electrical panel, and he jumped forward and stepped on her wrist.

She cried out and glared at him, and he said sternly. "Any more from you, and I'll just shoot you. You want to die?"

She bared her teeth in a snarl but relaxed and allowed herself to be handcuffed. "Good job, Special Agent," she said, her voice dripping with contempt. "You're a credit to the Service."

"And you're a terrorist."

He hauled her to her feet and pushed her ahead of him. When he walked into the cabin, he saw Jess sitting up and rubbing her head.

"I had to give her a smaller dose," Melina explained. "I figured you would probably come after me, so I saved most of it for you." She cast him a sultry smile and said, "Too bad you're such a badass."

"Laugh it up," Jake said, "It's all you have left. Gutierrez." The agent followed Mercer, frowning darkly at the latest terrorist they'd apprehended. "You're going to help Trent guard our prisoners. Take her to the relief cabin. I'll be there in a moment."

Gutierrez grabbed Melina and headed to the front, dragging the First Officer with him. "Let's go, *puta*," he spat. "And if you feel like giving me a reason, that's fine too."

Jake turned to Jess. "Are you all right?"

Jess smiled groggily and lifted a thumb. "Need a few minutes before I'm a hundred, but I'll be okay."

"Good. I hate to jump right into work, but as soon as you are okay, I want a full background suite on Captain Sontag. Three of our four crew have turned out to be terrorists, and I need to know if Ian's compromised as well."

"A-kay-o, *capitano*."

Jake left Jess and returned to the cockpit. Gutierrez was busy tying Melina to the chair. The terrorist continued to laugh, teasing Gutierrez by saying, "Do you like me tied up, Special Agent?"

"Gag her," Jake told Gutierrez, "as tightly as you want to."

"With pleasure, sir."

Jake knocked on the cockpit door and tapped his earpiece at the same time. "Trent, it's Mercer. Open up."

Trent did, gun drawn. He holstered his weapon when he saw Jake, and his eyes widened when he saw Melina. "Her too?" He met Jake's eyes and hooked a thumb back at Ian. "Is he—?"

"Jess is looking into it," Jake said quietly.

He hoped desperately that Ian would be clean. Jake didn't know the first thing about flying jet planes. He had flown helicopters once or twice in a pinch when he was in the Marine Corps, but he had never been certified as a pilot of any kind. If their pilot turned out to be a terrorist, too, they were in deep trouble.

"Captain Sontag, it turns out that Melina is a terrorist as well."

"What? Her too?"

Jake nodded. "I caught her fiddling with some controls at the rear of the airplane. If I were a betting man, I'd say she was responsible for throwing your navigational instruments out of wack."

"Jesus," Ian said. "What happens if…" he didn't finish the question.

"We can't let that happen," Jake said. "So Merrill's job is now to ensure you stay alive." He looked at Merrill. "You understand?"

"Yes, sir."

"And don't let anyone in here but me. Don't let Ian out, either. If he needs to take a piss, he can use the cockpit toilet. If he wants a snack, call me, and I'll bring it. Understand?"

Merrill frowned slightly. He knew he was in the hot seat for allowing Melina out of the cockpit. "Yes, sir."

"Good. No offense, by the way, Ian."

"None taken. Jesus Christ. I've known Melina for five years."

And I knew Drew for years.

"Are we on course now?"

"Yes, sir. Forty minutes until we rendezvous with the fighters."

"Can we see them on radar yet?"

"Not yet. They're stealth fighters, sir. They should be able to see us in ten minutes or so, though."

"All right. I want to know the moment we're in contact."

He turned and left the cockpit again, closing the door behind him before looking at Melina. "Melina, I don't need to tell you that things look bad for you. All three of you. We have the military waiting at Honolulu International Airport to respond instantly to any threats you've been trying to lead us to. We have an Air Force fighter escort on the way, along with a tanker. We're being monitored by AWACS, and they've discovered the decoy signal on the mainland. The jig is up.

"So here's the deal: you work with me, and I don't feel a need to call my buddies in the CIA and ask them if they want fresh meat for the prisons they run somewhere we're not allowed to know. Believe me when I tell you, you want to do time in a civilian prison, not one of their labs."

He reached forward and tore the tape off of Melina's mouth. It was pressed down tight. Gutierrez had done a thorough job.

Melina cried out as the tape was torn off. Her lips were red and puffy, and as she spoke, they began to welt. "I was willing to divert Air Force One and force it to blow up or crash into the ocean. Do you think I give a shit where I do time?"

"Torture is worse than death," Jake said, "to put a very blunt point on it. What about you two?" he asked the other two. "You guys feel like testing how effective the CIA's new drugs are?"

"You talk like a big man," Franz said, "but you're just a coward like all the rest."

"Cowards in control are the most dangerous people alive," Jake said. "So ease my fear. Tell me what I'm going to find when we land in Hawaii."

"Your downfall," Franz said. "Plain and simple. Your inevitable, complete downfall."

Jake nodded. "Gag Melina and Franz," he said.

"Ooh, I like it kinky," Melina teased.

Jake ignored the outburst and turned to Dana. "All right, Dana. Last chance. You feel like joining your buddies, or would you like to retain whatever meager amount of sanity you have left?"

Dana chuckled softly. She seemed the most depressed of the free. Jake hoped to use that. If he could convince her to give up hope, then maybe he could convince her to confide in him.

She met his eyes, and his hope died. "This ends the way it was always going to end," she said. "As Franz told you, the President's downfall was inevitable. All tyrants fall. You've been fighting for the losing side this entire time."

Jake sighed. "Well, I can't help delusion this strong. In that case, I'll just make sure that I get all three of you sent somewhere the CIA can use you best. Maybe you'll be lucky enough to die before things get too painful."

"You sound like a comic book villain," Dana said. "Everyone dies, and failure is a far more painful end than torture. Even if the CIA does have some division that specializes in torturing people, I'm not concerned. I'm ready to answer for my choices. Are you?"

Jake didn't dignify that with a response.

CHAPTER TEN

Jake stood over Jess, arms folded, a scowl on his face.

"Oh, Jake, it's so sweet of you to watch over me like this," Jess said, "but I'm afraid I work better when I don't have an angry bear huffing and puffing over me."

"Fine," Jake said. "I'll be in the cockpit."

"Hold your horses, dumbass," Jess said. "I'm just teasing."

"How can you tease at a time like this?" Jake said. "You were assaulted, and Air Force One was sabotaged again. How are you not… not…"

"Not freaking out like the world's ending? Maybe because I'm not a stress monster like you are. We've stopped them at every turn, Jake. We'll stop them again."

"I don't understand why they've left us alive. They talk about our downfall, about wanting to blow the plane up if we don't listen, but then they carefully inject us with enough sedative to put us to sleep for a few minutes with no lasting side effects? It makes no sense."

"When have terrorists ever made sense?"

"All the time. Twisted sense, but sense of some sort."

"Well, then this probably makes twisted sense of some sort. We just have to figure out what that is. And that's something I think I'm getting closer to discovering."

Jake turned toward her, "Yeah? What do you have?"

"Encoded communications between Dana and Melina and someone on the ground. They seem to have taken place shortly before takeoff."

"Who on the ground?"

"Not sure. I've narrowed it down to somewhere in Idaho, but I don't know where exactly yet."

"Somewhere in Idaho. Lovely."

"Feel free to take over if you feel you can do a better job," Jess quipped.

"I didn't mean it like that. I just… This is the first time I truly don't understand what's going on."

"Well, patience *kemo sabe*. We're getting closer."

Jake's earpiece buzzed. "Jake, it's Merrill. We've made contact with the fighter escort. They're requesting to talk to you."

"On my way." He turned to Jess. "Keep working on those communications. We need answers ASAP."

"You got it, *kemo sabe*."

"You can stop calling me that."

"I sure could."

Jake rolled his eyes, but he was in somewhat better spirits as he made his way to the cockpit. Jess's playfulness irritated him, but if her spirits were high enough that she could maintain a positive attitude, then maybe things weren't as bad as Jake thought they were.

Not that it could get much worse than flying a compromised Air Force One on three engines with multiple terrorists threatening him, his team and the President and his family.

He reached the cockpit and saw Ian's knuckles white around the control yoke. The captain turned to Jake and nearly collapsed with relief. "Diamond One, this is Air Force One. Special Agent Mercer is here to talk to you."

"Go ahead, Diamond One," Jake said.

Instead of answering, one of the escorts—an F-22 Raptor—flew in front of the cockpit upside down. They had flown ahead of the sunset, and the afternoon sun gleamed off of the stealth fighter. Jake nearly made eye contact with the helmeted pilot before the fighter jet broke away from the transport. Jake watched in awe as the stealth fighter did a barrel roll to right itself before positioning itself above and ahead of the left wing.

"Visual contact confirmed," a strange voice—Diamond One, Jake presumed—said over the radio. "Air Force One, continue on your present course. Tanker YF19226 will rendezvous with us in T-minus forty-four minutes. Upon refueling, we will proceed southeast toward Hickam Air Force Base."

"Negative, Diamond One," Jake interrupted. "Be advised, we have reports of a possible GPS-activated explosive device that will detonate if Air Force One lands anywhere other than Honolulu International Airport."

There was silence for a moment. Jake watched the F-22 as it effortlessly maintained its position relative to Air Force One. He couldn't see the second aircraft and assumed it was behind them. Even knowing that there was no way in hell the jets would shoot down Air Force One, the knowledge that two of the most advanced and capable fighter jets in the world were flying alongside them was a nerve-wracking experience. He could understand why Ian was nervous.

Unless, of course, Ian was nervous because he was also a terrorist.

The radio crackled. "Roger, Air Force One. Destination confirmed as Honolulu International Airport. Be advised, the Airport will be closed to civilian traffic within two hours, and the runway will be cleared within four."

"That works for me," Jake said. "Captain, how long to Hawaii once we're refueled?"

"Seven hours."

"Outstanding."

Eight more hours. Eight more hours, and they would be on the ground. Christ, had it only been eight hours since they took off?

"Be advised," Diamond One said, and Jake thought he could detect a trace of reluctance in the pilot's voice. "We are instructed to shoot Air Force One down should the plane attempt to fly toward a civilian or military target."

Ian stiffened, and his fingers tightened further around the yoke. Jake blinked in surprise. "Shoot us down? The President is on board, Diamond One. Repeat, President Jackson is on board Air Force One."

"Understood, sir," Diamond One said, "Nevertheless, I have my orders. Is this a secure channel?"

"No, turn to 165.335"

He tapped his earpiece and said, "Diamond One, do you read me?"

"Loud and clear. Listen, Special Agent, I'm not any happier about this than you are, but this is a post 9/11 world. If we find out you're on a collision course, then we have to assume the President is already dead, and you're threatening American lives."

Jake sighed. "Understood, Diamond One. Please allow us every chance before you take that measure."

"Of course, sir. Switching to the public channel now."

Jake tapped his earpiece, and Diamond One said, "For the remainder of this flight, keep this channel clear in case of emergency."

"You got it," Ian replied. "I mean, yes, sir."

"Diamond One, out."

Ian released a deep breath and said, "Christ, I hate this."

"Just a few more hours, Captain," Jake said. "Hold it together and get us on the ground."

"I'll do that, and then I'm tendering my resignation effective immediately and going to work for a civilian carrier. No offense, but this terrorist crap isn't my cup of tea."

"I don't blame you," Jake said.

He left Ian and Merrill and returned to the main cabin. Jess waved him down when he arrived, which was unnecessary since he was already heading to her.

"What do you have for me?"

"Good news," she said. "Ian is clean. The bad news is that the other three are clean too. Not so much as a traffic ticket among them."

Jake sighed. "I guess they would have to be clean to be selected to fly Air Force One. Any news on the origin of the EMP attack?"

"Nothing yet. Wherever it's from, it's not showing up on any Secret Service or DoD lists. I'm trying to get a hold of the NSA to see if they have records, but my buddy at the NSA is on vacation, so I have to go through red tape."

"Red tape? Does no one understand that the President is on board this aircraft?"

"They do, and they also understand that there was a false Air Force One chatting away with Air Traffic Control without a care in the world. They're being cautious."

Jake sighed and rubbed his temples. "Jesus. Well, keep looking. I still don't understand what these guys want, and I'd really like to not fly right into their hands."

"Well, the military is clearing the airport, right?"

"The military cleared this plane too," Jake countered, "and so did we. I don't know that I trust anyone's assurances right now."

"Trust mine. We *will* find whoever's responsible for this. I promise you."

Jake met Jess's eyes and was surprised to find that he actually did take a little comfort in her confidence. "Thank you. When we get home, I owe you a steak dinner."

"Replace steak dinner with luxury sports car, and you might be a little closer to the truth."

Jake chuckled. "I'll see what I can do."

"Wait, can you really buy me a sports car?"

"Sure. I saw a nice RC Porsche on sale at Walmart for a hundred bucks. I'll even gift wrap it for you."

Jess smiled sweetly and lifted her finger at him as he made his way to the President's stateroom. He chuckled again and reached the

President's room in a slightly better mood than before. "Coulson? It's Mercer. I'm coming in."

"Roger that, sir."

The door opened, and Jake walked in to see the President and his family laughing and smiling with each other. Carrie's smile faded upon seeing Jake, but the fact that she was able to enjoy herself was a good sign.

"Hey, baby!" Sheila said.

She leaped up and rushed him, planting a kiss on his lips before he could stop her. He tried to push her away, but she clung more tightly, and he resigned himself to enduring the kiss.

Well, enduring was the wrong word. Sheila kissed him deeply and passionately, and even in front of two agents and Sheila's parents, Jake couldn't help but enjoy it. Still, he wasn't particularly enthused, knowing that Sheila was mostly doing this to upset her mother.

Finally, Sheila pulled away, and Jake said, "I have an update. We've made contact with the fighter escort. We're on our way to rendezvous with the tanker. Aircraft systems are… well, the flight systems are good. We don't have satellite navigation anymore, but the F-22s do, and we're still on track to arrive at Honolulu in just about eight hours."

"Great," Bryan said. "I'd like to say something to the pilots."

Jake frowned. "I'm sorry, sir. The situation is still volatile. I need you to remain here where it's safe."

"If you insist, I'll stay," Bryan replied, "but those pilots have put their lives on the line for us. I'd like to thank them for their service."

Jake looked at Coulson and Roberts, both of whom returned blank stares. They seemed happy to know that they weren't responsible for this decision, and Jake couldn't blame them.

He sighed and said, "I'm sorry, sir. We… we're holding the terrorists in the relief cabin. I can't let them see you. They're restrained, but…" he sighed again and tapped his earpiece. "Jess, can you tap into the channel our escorts are using? The President would like to speak with them."

"Sure. One moment."

"I'm handing you to the President. Let him know when he's connected to them."

Jake handed Bryan his headset. The President smiled and said, "Hi, Jess. All right." After a brief pause, he said, "Diamond One, Diamond Two. This is the President speaking. I wanted to thank you for coming over to help us out. My family and I are very grateful.

"I know the past year has been trying for this nation. We find ourselves faced with a truly unprecedented threat. I thank you for your resolve and your patience as we show the world that the United States will never cow in the face of terrorism. The nation owes you a debt of gratitude. I owe you a debt of gratitude."

Jake had a lot of opinions about Bryan both as a friend and a president. Not all of them were positive. But that brief speech reminded him why the man had won election twice, the second time after multiple terrorist attacks had left thousands dead. He took the headset back, and when Bryan said, "Thank you," Jake meant it with his whole heart when he said, "You're welcome."

His good mood lasted exactly as long as it took him to set the headphone on his head. "Jake," Jess said, "Please don't hate me, but I have some bad news."

"All right. I'll be right there."

"Bring Coulson with you?"

Jake's brow furrowed. "All right. Coulson? With me, please. I need your help with something."

"Of course, sir."

The two of them left the room. They reached the cabin to find Jess standing with her gun drawn.

"Jess? What's—"

Jake's question was cut off when Coulson landed a lightning-fast blow to his groin. He doubled over, gasping from the pain, and watched as Coulson grabbed Jess's wrist and twisted her gun out of her hand. He aimed the weapon at Jess, then looked behind them at the hallway and swore.

He sprinted toward the back of the plane, narrowly avoiding the gunfire sent his way by Trent and Gutierrez, who watched, shell-shocked, from the open door of the relief cabin.

Jake could hear the laughter of the terrorists as he went to Jess.

"I'm all right," Jess said. "Go after him."

CHAPTER ELEVEN

Jake tapped his earpiece. "Remain at your posts everyone. I'm going alone. I'll keep this channel on in case I get hit, but I don't want to risk that Coulson's trying to draw everyone away from their duties."

"That *hijo de perra*," Gutierrez growled. "I'm going to tear his *cojones* off and shove them down his throat."

"He doesn't have *cojones*," Trent said, a rare breach of professionalism for the seasoned agent. "He's a coward like every terrorist."

"Enough," Jake snapped. "I'm as pissed as all of you, but we need to stay sharp. Merrill, I want that cockpit door sealed. Roberts, same with the President's stateroom. Patel, is Chef Trumbull in his quarters or the galley?"

"The galley, sir. He's preparing breakfast for the President and his family."

"Then he stays in the galley. So do you, and so does the breakfast."

"He won't like that, sir."

"I don't give a rat's ass what he likes! Secure the galley, Patel."

"Yes, sir."

"Ian, do you have an update for me?"

"We're twenty-eight minutes from reaching the tanker. They have us on radar now."

"Wonderful. Business as usual for you, but if you see anything fishy on your instruments at all, I want to know about it. I'm almost certain Coulson is trying to sabotage us again." A thought occurred to him. "Are there backup systems you can reroute flight controls to? Anywhere that Coulson can't access from the back room?"

Ian responded brightly. "Yes! Of course! I'll do that right now. Can't do anything about air conditioning, so he can make it unpleasantly hot if he wants to, but that's about it."

"Good. Get it done. Jess? Can you track Coulson?"

"Watch out!" his partner cried.

Jake instinctively threw himself to the left. Unfortunately, that was where Coulson was. Fortunately, that worked out to Jake's advantage. His shoulder struck Coulson in the solar plexus, and the man grunted and fell to the floor. They were in the quarters that Trent and Merrill would have shared if the flight hadn't gone straight to hell. That gave both men about thirty square feet to work with.

Jake got to his feet and reached for his weapon but abandoned the plan when Coulson lunged at him with a knife. He caught the younger man's wrist and tried to disarm him, but Coulson grabbed the back of Jake's head and drove his knee into Jake's midsection.

Jake managed to get his right hand up to protect himself, but most of the force of the blow found its way to his liver. He gasped and fell to the floor. Coulson shook his wrist and yanked it free of Jake's grasp. Instantly, he brought the knife down again.

Jake chopped up at Coulson's wrist. The move was designed to briefly weaken Coulson's grip and get him to drop the knife, but Coulson held on. Jake grabbed his wrist again, and Coulson threw a hard left hook. Jake stiff-armed Coulson's bicep to block the shot, but he was on his knees, and Coulson planted his foot on Jake's chest and pushed back, tearing his arms free again.

Jake rushed Coulson. Once more grabbing Coulson's knife hand and forcing the traitor against the wall of the cabin. Coulson grunted with effort, resisting Jake's attempts to bring him to the ground. Jake pressed hard, twisting and trying to bring Coulson off balance.

With a rapid spin, Coulson lifted Jake off of his feet and threw him to the ground. He planted his knee on Jake's throat and pressed down hard. The pressure on Jake's windpipe was extraordinary. If he didn't move quickly, Coulson would crush it, and Jake would die.

He spun, bringing his knee up and driving it into Coulson's back. Coulson gasped and arched his back. The pressure softened on Jake's neck, and he managed to extricate his head and drive his knee into Coulson's back again.

Coulson cried out, then glared at Jake. He snarled and planted his knee on Jake again, this time on his solar plexus. Jake gasped, struggling to take in breath while Coulson calmly worked the knife slowly but surely from Jake's grasp. He pulled it free and drove it down again. Again Jake blocked his wrist.

"God*damn*it!" Coulson growled. He swung the knife in a backward arc, aiming for Jake's thigh. Jake brought his left leg up, and the knife sailed under his leg instead. Jake bucked his hips, trying to pin Coulson's hand to the wall, but the agent twisted free and shifted his weight hire on Jake's chest.

That was a mistake. Jake lifted his legs up. He swung his right leg around Coulson's throat, hooking it with his other leg. He flexed, and the startles Coulson fell backward. Jake used the momentum of the fall to rise to a sitting position.

Coulson lifted the knife up and stabbed, and this time, Jake was a split second too slow in blocking the blow. The knife buried itself in his thigh, and he cried out as pain shot through him like a lightning bolt.

Coulson grinned and started to twist the blade, sending scintillating shocks up and down Jake's left side.

Jake forced himself to stand and rolled Coulson onto his stomach. He drove his knee down into Coulson's back and heard something crack. Coulson gasped and began to tremble on the ground.

Jake stumbled backwards and looked at his knife wound while the stricken agent shivered and jerked in front of him.

"You… you bastard!" Coulson finally said. "You broke my back!"

"Should've aimed higher," Jake said. He tapped his earpiece. "Gutierrez, come help me."

"On my way. Are you all right, boss?"

Jake looked down at the knife sticking out of his leg. "I might need medical."

"Shit. Okay, I'll take over for Patel and send him instead."

"Fine with me," Jake said.

"You're all going to fall," Coulson hissed. "All of you. Your days are numbered, asshole!"

"A higher number than yours," Jake countered. "I would stop trying to move if I were you. Your back's only out of joint, not broken, but if you keep messing with that herniated disc, you'll sever your spinal cord."

Coulson glared at Jake, but he retained enough self-preservation to comply. A moment later, Patel walked in. He trained his gun on Coulson, then looked at Jake. "He's incapacitated?"

"Yep. A herniated disc, maybe more than one."

"Ah."

Patel planted his foot on Coulson's back and shoved hard. Coulson screamed, but when his scream died down, he could move again. He rolled over, but any thought he might have had about fighting more ended when hc saw both Jake's and Patel's guns pointed at his head.

"Roll back onto your stomach," Jake said. "Patel here is going to tie you up nice and cozy. Then he's going to take care of my leg. Then you and I are going to have a conversation. Actually, we'll talk while Patel works."

Patel holstered his weapon and began binding Coulson, using his and Jake's handcuffs and tying together the sheets of the two bunks before using them to tie both sets of handcuffs together behind Coulson's back.

"Who are you?" Jake asked.

"A patriot," Coulson replied. "Just like Dana, Franz and Melina."

"Wait, you guys are using your real names?"

"Of course," Coulson said. "Why would a patriot hide his nature?"

Patel chuckled and shook his head, continuing to tighten Coulson's bonds.

"Well, you definitely showed your nature. Tell me something, Coulson. Actually, tell me everything. None of this makes any sense to me."

"That's why you're still blind."

Jake sighed. "Okay, I'll rephrase. Tell me everything, or I'll have Patel break your back for good this time."

"Why do you keep fighting this?" Coulson asked. "Free people will always defeat tyrants. It's inevitable."

"You make a hell of a philosopher, Coulson. Too bad you decided to go into terrorism instead."

Patel moved over to Jake and looked at the knife. "Good thing for you it's just a flesh wound. Slipped in between the tensor fasciae latae and the rectus femoris."

"I have no idea what you said," Jake replied, "but I'm glad I'm not dying."

"Nope." Patel yanked the knife out, and Jake cried out.

"Come on," Patel said. "Go to the main cabin and take your pants off. I'll drag Hamlet the Horrible out behind you, then dress your leg. You'll last a minute or two without bleeding out."

"Good to know."

Jake limped back to the main cabin and stripped his pants. Jess watched him, and Jake said, "You mind giving me a little privacy?" Jess lifted her eyes to his, and when Jake saw the fear in her expression, he sighed. "Sorry. Just a little touchy."

"Getting stabbed in the leg will do that. You're okay, though?"

"That's what our resident doctor tells me. He could use some work on his bedside manner."

Patel walked into the cabin a moment later. He dropped Coulson on his face unceremoniously, and the traitor cried out as his nose smashed onto the ground.

Patel opened a compartment in the wall of the cabin and pulled out a first aid kit. "We'll have you sewn up in a moment," he said. "Well, bound up. The sewing part will have to wait until I have more time, but it's a clean wound, so you might not even need stitches."

"Wonderful."

As Patel worked, Jess said, "I have some news, but I don't know if I should wait until tinywiener over there is put somewhere."

Coulson rolled onto his side. "You were going to tell Jake that the facility that disabled Air Force One's radio and navigation was a CIA facility in the Idaho Rocky Mountains." Jess's eyes widened in shock, and Coulson chuckled. "Yeah, it doesn't matter now. You're all dead anyway. We're all dead."

"If that were true, you wouldn't have agreed to save your life a minute ago," Jake countered.

"What can I say? I want to be around to witness the felling of the tyrant."

"If you wanted to feel the tyrant, you would have tried to shoot him or crash the plane. I don't think that's what you really want."

Coulson laughed and turned to Jake. "You don't get it? Still? The President isn't the tyrant we're after, Jake."

The three agents—the non-traitorous ones—blinked in surprise. Coulson laughed again. "Hey, we'll get the President two. Kill two Caligulas with one knife, so to speak. But Air Force One is just the vessel, not the target. Not the true target anyway."

"Who's the true target?"

"Uh uh uh," Coulson said. "I wouldn't want to reveal the ending. I'll give you a hint, though. You've been told this before, but I'll say it again. There's more than one bomb on this plane."

Jake's eyes narrowed. "So the plane will explode upon touchdown."

"The bomb will go off when the time is right," Coulson replied. "It's already too late. But keep trying to fight. It's amusing."

Jake looked at Jess. Her lips were set in a thin line, a clear sign she was worried.

As well she should be.

In a way, this was Trident's best plan. There was nowhere to run. There was nowhere to hide. They were in a flying office building thousands of feet in the air. The only way out was down, and the only way down was to detonate a bomb.

They were already dead.

CHAPTER TWELVE

"Getting crowded in here," Merrill pointed out.

He was right. The relief cabin was designed for two people. At the moment, there were four bound prisoners and two Secret Service agents. Jake was forced to stand just outside the door to talk to his agents.

"You're right. Let's escort the prisoners to the unused cabins in the rear of the plane. The first cabin's small, but it's still bigger than this one. You and Gutierrez will keep them under guard."

Gutierrez gestured at Coulson. "We could always just toss this one out of the plane and make some more room."

"I appreciate your feelings, Gutierrez, but we need to maintain a professional demeanor even under trying circumstances."

Gutierrez didn't look happy with the direction, but he nodded and said, "Yes, sir."

Jake turned to his prisoners. "That being said, our profession will require us to take drastic measures should we deem them necessary. Give my agents any trouble—bound or otherwise—and you might find yourself taking the trip Special Agent Gutierrez just advised."

"We are to die anyway, win or lose," Franz pointed out, "so what does it matter?"

"I wouldn't give up on your future just yet," Jake replied. "I intend for all of you to live a very, very long life."

"Good luck with that," Coulson muttered.

"All right," Jake said. "Let's get them out of here."

Despite their bravado, the prisoners were perfectly compliant as the agents escorted them to the rear of the plane, no doubt motivated by Gutierrez's dark scowl and the loving way he fingered the trigger of his handgun.

Once the prisoners were moved to their new home, Jake made his way back to the cockpit. Trent opened the door for him, and Jake took the copilot's seat. "How are we looking, Captain?"

"Good so far. Getting that extra load of fuel allowed me to slow down to a more comfortable speed for three engines. Not that we were likely to have any problems, but the extra peace of mind is nice. It also gives us an extra hour or so to figure out the bomb."

"That's actually what I wanted to talk to you about. I'm going to start looking for the bomb in earnest. We have the prisoners secured in a locked cabin, and Jess's scans haven't been able to reveal anything, so we're going an old-fashioned compartment by compartment search. I've heard several strong allusions from our prisoners that suggest the bomb will go off upon touchdown no matter where we land.

"Even in Honolulu?"

"Even in Honolulu. So my question to you is, how long can Air Force One stay in the air with midair refueling?"

Ian sighed. "Under ideal conditions, we can stay airborne for up to a week. Missing an engine? Well, we're making things risky if we stay up longer than twenty-four hours."

"How long have we been airborne now?"

"About eleven hours."

"Lucky number thirteen. We'll go with that."

"What about having the President and his family jump?" Trent suggested. "We could head to land and fly at ten thousand feet. We'll put them in chutes, and once they're offloaded, we ditch the plane in the ocean."

"Wouldn't that kill all of us?" Ian asked.

"My thought was that Chef Trumbull would jump with the President and his family along with the rest of the agents. Then, you would get us headed back over the ocean. Once you have that set, you turn the controls over to me and jump yourself. I fly the plane over the ocean."

"Do you know how to fly?"

"Doesn't matter. I get to open waters and push the nose down."

"So you're talking about sacrificing your own life?"

Trent shrugged. "I mean, I can take a chute and try to make my way to the back of the plane and jump out the rear exit, but... yeah, probably." Ian stared in horror, and Trent smiled. "That's the job."

Jake frowned. Aside from losing Trent, a sacrifice he very much didn't want to make, doing that would mean that all of the terrorists die and they have no one left to interrogate to figure out what this was all about.

"We're saving that for an absolute last resort," Jake finally said, *And I'm the one flying the plane in that scenario*, he didn't say. "If we can stay up for thirteen more hours, that's thirteen hours to scour the plane and find the bomb. These guys are slick, but they're not that slick. We've caught and imprisoned all four of them. We can find a way out of this. Don't lose hope."

Trent grinned. "You should be a motivational speaker, boss. You're wasted on the Service."

Jake returned his smile. "I'll take that under advisement, Special Agent. Captain Sontag, can you contact Diamond One, please?'

Ian tapped the radio, and Jake said, "Diamond One, this is Air Force One."

"Go ahead, Air Force One."

"I'm afraid there's been a complication. We now have good reason to believe that the explosive device aboard Air Force One is rigged to explode upon contact with the surface regardless of destination. With this in mind, my agents and I are going to conduct a thorough search of the aircraft. If we can find and disarm the device, we'll proceed to the nearest convenient military airfield. If not, then we'll descend to ten thousand feet and offload the President and his family via parachute. Once that's done, one agent will remain on board and ditch the aircraft into the ocean."

There was a brief silence on the other end before Diamond One said, "Roger that, Air Force One. How long can you stay airborne?"

"Captain Sontag tells me thirteen more hours."

"Understood. Our birds will need to land before then. We'll fly ahead of you and contact Hickam Air Force Base to send replacement escorts. ASAP. Continue on your present course. Good luck, Air Force One."

"Thank you, Diamond One."

Night had finally caught up to them, and Jake watched in awe as the afterburners of the two stealth fighters lit up, propelling them ahead of Air Force One.

"Too bad we can't just put the President on another aircraft and watch our boys go to work," Trent said.

That wasn't a professional comment, but Jake didn't feel the urge to correct him. "As you were, boys. I'm going to talk to the chef and see if we can get some coffee."

***

Fifteen minutes later, Jake sat next to Jess and handed her a steaming mug of something Chef Trumbull called Arabian Mokka. Jess took the cup gratefully and sipped even more gratefully. She rolled her eyes in the back of her head and said, "Oh God, this is perfection. Thank you, buddy."

"Anytime, partner. Do you have any updates for me?"

"A couple good ones. So that CIA facility in Idaho? Well, the CIA just raided it this morning."

"The CIA raided their own facility?"

"For good reason, I'm afraid. The operatives stationed there were gone and are presumed dead. The facility was transmitting automatically under the directions of a computer installed within the past week. They were able to recover security footage from some hidden cameras in the facility, though."

"Anything interesting?"

Jess turned her laptop to reveal an image of a familiar face. "He only showed his face for two seconds, but that was enough."

"It sure was."

The face staring back at the two of them belonged to former Marine Andrew McNeill. This confirmed that this was a Trident operation. Jake's blood boiled as he saw his best friend once more putting innocent lives at risk to help a terrorist.

"The rest of the video shows him setting up the computer then leaving the facility," Jess continued.

"It was empty when he arrived?"

"Yes."

"And they presume their operatives were killed?"

"I think they plan on finding their operatives and… taking care of business themselves."

"Ah. Well, I can't say I blame them."

"Really? I mean, I get that they're traitors, but you don't think that we're stooping to their level?"

"We haven't killed innocent civilians, so no, I don't think so. I think that when people are willing to use violence to hurt the innocent, the innocent need to be willing to use violence to defend themselves."

Jess lowered her eyes. "Maybe. You're probably right. It just… I don't know. It just sucks."

"It does," Jake agreed. After a moment of silence, he said, "You said you had another update for me?"

"Yes. I think I know why Hawaii is such a big deal."

"Oh?"

"Do you remember that defense contractor who was killed a few days before we left Washington?"

"Kline?"

"Yeah. It turns out that his company has a facility in Honolulu International Airport."

CHAPTER THIRTEEN

Jake knocked on the door to the cabin where the prisoners were being kept. "Merrill? Gutierrez? It's Mercer."

Merrill opened the door, and Jake walked in to see his prisoners groggy and trying to find a comfortable position to sleep, no easy task when one was hogtied. That was good. The more tired they were, the more prone they would be to suggestion.

Jess had identified Coulson as the one most likely to feel sympathy. He had started with the Secret Service actually intending to do good, as far as his background showed. It wasn't until the Trident attack in Washington when Bard gave his speech about needing to give warmongerers a taste of their own medicine that he began to show signs of concerning opinions and attitudes. If Jake could remind him that the point was to help people, not hurt them, then maybe Coulson would be willing to tell Jake what he knew.

But first, Jake wanted to interview Dana. She was the leader and the one least likely to bend. He wanted to give the impression that they were talking to each terrorist individually and not singling Coulson out.

He reached for Dana and lifted the woman off the ground. Dana grunted as she was pulled out of near sleep. She glared at Jake and Jake ripped the duct tape off of her mouth.

"Ow! Oh, you fucking asshole!"

"Oh yeah. That's me. Merrill, take her ankle cuffs off. Gutierrez, if she flinches, shoot her."

Gutierrez immediately leveled his weapon at Dana's temple. "You got it, boss."

Dana glared at the angry agent, but her eyes showed that she knew better than to provoke him, and she behaved while Merrill removed her ankle cuffs. She sighed with relief as she extended her legs and twisted her hips. "Look at that," she mocked. "I've been promoted to human being."

"Oh yeah. We've been so barbaric."

"Screw you."

Jake led Dana to the cabin immediately behind them. The insulation would probably keep the sounds of their voices from reaching the others, but if Coulson could overhear a little of what Jake had to say, it might get him thinking.

He sat Dana on one of the bunks and sat on the opposite bunk. “Okay, Dana. We went ahead and looked you up. Pristine criminal record, so nice job keeping everything hidden. Very interesting college history, though. Looks like you were a card-carrying pacifist for a while. What changed?”

“I grew up and realized that peace doesn’t inspire people, it just makes them feel comfortable. If you want peace, you have to get rid of people who want war.”

"Ah, yes. Peace through violence. Makes sense."

“Whatever you need to tell yourself. I don’t feel ashamed of any of my choices.”

“Always good to live with no regrets. Anyway, why Kline specifically?”

Dana blinked, clearly surprised to learn that Jake knew about that. “What do you mean?”

“Ooh, playing stupid. Not smart. We don’t like that. Want to try again?”

Jake could see the war in Dana’s eyes. Did she admit to her motives for a chance to show the imperialist pig how much more righteous she was, or did she keep her mouth shut and prevent them from learning whatever it was they were trying to learn?

In the end, pride won out, as Jake knew it would. She lifted her chin haughtily and said, “Kline was the worst of his kind. He grew fat off of the blood of innocent victims but lacked the courage to pick up the sword himself.”

“So why work with Bard? Bard’s the same kind of terrorist. He hires other people to do his dirty work for him.”

“Bard fights imperialists, just like us. Besides, when you lack power, you have to make alliances. It’s the nature of our mission.”

“Got it. One last question: how do you sleep at night?”

She scoffed. “Like a baby. When I’m not being tortured by imperialists and warmongers.”

“So it doesn’t bother you that a lot of innocent civilians are going to die when you destroy Kline’s building in Honolulu?”

“They’re not innocent. They work for the warmonger. They’re as guilty as any soldier.”

“What about the people in the terminal nearby? The airport workers who aren’t trying to enrich Kline?”

"The airport lends the warmonger their land. The people who work for the airport are guilty by association."

"Boy. That's a lot of people. Just out of curiosity, who *doesn't* deserve to be killed for the cause of peace?"

"You can mock me all you want. I'm secure in my cause."

"Sure. All right. Thank you."

"That's it?"

"That's it. I was hoping you'd tell me where the bomb was so I could disarm it and innocents didn't have to die, but it sounds like you're really good at convincing yourself it's okay to kill people so other people don't kill people. I won't waste my time anymore."

He yanked her to her feet, and she gasped. "Ow! For *fuck's* sake!"

"Act like a decent person, and I'll treat you with decency."

"Oh, screw you!"

Jake returned her to the cabin, and Merrill and Gutierrez bound and gagged her. "Okay, Coulson," Jake said. "You're up next."

Jake pulled him to his feet. Coulson grimaced as Jake tugged on his shoulder, but he said nothing. Merrill uncuffed his ankle shackles as before while Gutierrez waited patiently for a chance to use his weapon. Fortunately for Coulson, he declined to give Gutierrez an excuse.

Jake led him to the same room and sat him down on the bed. Coulson didn't meet his eyes. That was a good sign. The guilt was getting to him.

Jake met his eyes and paused for a second before asking, "What happened, Dave?"

Coulson's brow furrowed, but he didn't say anything."

"We looked up your record. I mean, we know your Secret Service record, and it's exemplary. That's why you're here to begin with. We only entrust the President's safety to the most honorable of our agents. But even before that, you were a good guy. Honors in high school, top of your criminal justice class in college, and very active in your support of law enforcement and servicemen and women. Up until a year ago, you were the poster child for a law-abiding citizen. So what happened?"

Coulson didn't answer. Jake was about to press further when Coulson finally spoke. "Did you ever actually listen to Bard? When he was talking during the White House attack?"

"Of course I did. I always listen to everything terrorists have to say."

“But did you listen, or did you just look for clues that could help you arrest him?”

“Why don’t you tell me what you heard?”

Coulson shrugged. “He made sense. You’re right about me, Mercer. I’m not a violent person. I don’t like hurting people.”

“You nearly killed me.”

“Yeah, but… we can’t just wait for the government to change. We can’t just keep protesting peacefully and hope that the powers that be will lay down their arms and stop oppressing people. It will never happen. If we want change in the world, then we have to bring that change about. I hate that we have to use violence to do it, but that’s all violent people understand.”

"You realize, though, that a lot of people who aren't violent are going to die when this plane lands, right? I don't mean us. I mean people on the ground, people who aren't violent and aren't working for violent people. Passengers who are just traveling, airport workers trying to feed their families: a lot of those people will die. You have a niece, right?" Coulson frowned and didn't respond. "How would you like your niece to die in an airport bombing? Would you accept it if the people who hurt her said, 'Well, I'm very sorry, Dave, but you see, there was an arms dealer in the same airport as her, and we just had to blow up the entire airport to be sure.'?"

“That’s…”

“Different?”

Coulson’s gaze fell. His shoulders slumped, and Jake could see that he was getting through to him.

“I think you know better than that, Dave. It’s only different because it’s other people’s families, not yours.”

Coulson sniffed and shook his head. “What are we supposed to do, then? We just let them keep starting wars? We just let people keep getting murdered? We just, what, hold up signs and wait for their shame to kick in? We can’t keep doing it. From your perspective, Bard is a murderer, but you said it yourself: this is your country, and these are your people. So yeah, people who hurt them are evil. But what about people in the Middle East? What about people in Africa and South America? What about the people we hurt, the people our President and our government hurt? I’ll bet you if you ask someone in Syria grieving the loss of their father because of a U.S. airstrike who the bad guys are, they’ll point their fingers right back at us. Why are we any better than they are?”

"So you killed Kline. Good for you. You got the bad guy. Why are you going after innocent people?"

"The people who work for him aren't innocent."

"Well, then, neither are you. You've worked to protect the President for seven years."

"I know. I'm making up for that now."

Jake felt a touch of frustration. Coulson's walls were tougher than he expected them to be. "Dave, I'm asking you to think about this one thing right now. Please think about this one attack you're planning. In a few hours, this plane lands in Honolulu, and then what? You taxi it to Kline's building and hope that a bunch of passengers who are just looking to catch a plane home don't happen to be too close? Or do you just sweep that all under the "it's for the cause" rug and look the other way?"

"Well, we wouldn't have to do this if people would just stop!"

Coulson lifted his eyes to Jake, tears streaming down his cheeks. Jake couldn't drum up any sympathy for him. *What a fucking child. That's all you are. That's all any of you are. Just children throwing tantrums, too selfish and stupid to see past your own damned noses.*

Out loud, he said, "Dave, you keep trying to make this about philosophy. It's not. It's about people. Real people who will die if you let it happen. Tell me where the bomb is so I can disarm it, and you don't have to have their deaths on your conscience."

"Oh, man." Coulson's head slumped forward, and his chest hitched. "Jesus, I just want this to stop."

"So help me stop it. Tell me where the bomb is. Tell me, so we can stop it now, you and I."

"I mean, I want it *all* to stop! All the fighting! All the killing! All of it!"

"This won't stop it, Dave. Look at history. You guys aren't the first terrorist group to try bombing buildings. It's been done many times before. Has it worked?"

That finally got through to Coulson. He met Jake's eyes, and the defeat Jake saw was almost as good as repentance.

"It's in the hold," he whispered. "It's in a padlocked suitcase. That's all I know."

CHAPTER FOURTEEN

Jess looked somberly at Jake as he checked his gear one final time. He smiled at her and said, "What the hell's with that look? You've seen me go into way worse situations than this."

She managed a smile that looked about as real as Bard's loyalty to the Secret Service. "I know. It's just something about being in an airplane over open water." She shivered. "It's claustrophobia on top of fear of drowning on top of isolation on top of why does it always have to be you? Shouldn't it be me? I know technology way better than you do."

"That's exactly why I need you here. I need you to monitor electrical pulses. The bomb is in a padlocked compartment, which means I can't see if what I'm doing is going to trigger the bomb. You can. So you need to guide me from afar."

"Why don't I ever get to do the sexy jobs that earn medals?"

"I'll give you a medal for this."

She rolled her eyes. "Ha ha. I already deserve a medal for putting up with you."

"I'll give you two medals." Jess tried again with a smile and enjoyed a similar amount of success. "Come on," he said, "at least I'm not being ravaged by a super virus this time."

"That's not funny."

"I'm not joking. I can't tell you how happy I am to be physically fit this time around."

She chuckled and slapped his chest. "Be careful."

"When am I not careful?"

She gave him a dry look and didn't respond.

Jake tapped his earpiece. "Merrill, you're in charge while I'm in the hold. Stay with the prisoners for now, but if anything requires immediate attention, you're my guy, all right?"

"Yes, sir. Be careful, sir."

"Jesus, what's with all the sentiment? I'll be fine, guys."

"Of course, sir. I just overheard Gutierrez say he's going to share your internet browser history with Sheila if you die. I just don't want that to happen to you."

Jake and Jess both laughed out loud at that. "You're a true friend, Merrill. Tell Gutierrez I'll have Jess email his history to his mother."

"Hey, that's messed up," Gutierrez said. "My mother never did anything to you."

"That you know of."

"That's *really* messed up."

Jake chuckled. "All right, kids. I'm going in. You all behave and listen to Mr. Merrill while I'm gone."

"I'm heading straight for the cookie jar," Gutierrez said.

"Good luck with that," Patel chimed in. "Chef and I already ate 'em all."

"Oh, now that's the most messed up of all. No cookies for your brother? That's cold, Arjun."

The ladder to the hold was just in front of the galley. Jake opened the hatch and started down. The hold was pressurized but not heated, and Jake was glad for the jacket he wore. Automatic lights came on as he descended, and he could see the entire hold from bow to stern.

He was grateful that the plane was only lightly populated right now. Other than the President's luggage, food supplies and a few extra cases of ammunition and supplies for Jake and his agents, the hold was empty.

That made it easy to locate the bomb. The device was contained, as Coulson said, in a padlocked box. It looked to be about one foot by two feet by two feet and was bolted to the floor of the hold. In a civilian airplane of this age, they wouldn't have been able to do that without compromising the airplane, but in Air Force One, the hold had an inner wall separate from the hull of the aircraft.

Jake wondered wryly if the designers of the plane had anticipated bombs being drilled into the floor when they built the plane.

"Okay, Jess," Jake said. "I'm at the bomb. I'm going to scan it with your wand thingy."

Jess laughed. "Wand thingy?"

"You know, the scanner thing. The stick you gave me—"

"I know what you're talking about, dummy. I just… wand thingy?"

Jake rolled his eyes. "Focus."

"Hey, does Sheila like playing with your wand thingy?"

Jake sighed and pulled the scanning tool from the pouch attached to his belt. He waved it over the box, and a red light began to flash.

"Keep waving it until it turns green."

Jake obliged, and a moment later, the red flashing light turned into a solid green one. “Okay. It’s green now.”

“Well, do you want the good news or the bad news?”

“Bad news.”

"The detonator is indeed connected to the lock itself. If you screw up the code to disarm it, then bye-bye, Air Force One."

“Lovely. Well, at least we saw it coming.”

“I love your ability to look on the bright side.”

“The side would be a lot brighter if the good news is that you know how to disarm it anyway.”

"Just call me Bright Eyes!" Jess said cheerfully. "Okay, put the scanner next to the opening. This next part is very important. Slowly turn the dials one at a time until the light turns green. Go slowly, but don't stop. If you stop, boom. If you overshoot, keep going in the same direction until you reach the number again. Don't pull back or kablooey."

“You have a lot of words for explosions.”

“I have a lot of experience with wand thingies.”

“All right. Didn’t want to know that.”

“Well, now you do. So, are you going to start, or do you need me to come down and help you?”

“I’m starting.”

Jake slowly moved the first of six wheels away from him. With each click, the scanning tool flashed red once. When Jake reached the number six, the tool flashed green.

“Okay, the first one’s done. Do I take it away, and then put it back, or do I just go on to the next wheel?”

“Never take it away after it’s in. Keep it there until it’s finished.”

“Got it. Moving on to the second number.”

He turned the wheel, and the light flashed green right on one. He tried to stop, but the wheel moved to two, and the tool flashed red again.

“Shit.”

“Keep turning. Do *not* stop. It’s okay, there’s no timer on this detonator. Take your time and get back to one.”

Jake continued to slowly turn the wheel until it showed one again. The tool flashed green, and he moved on to the third number.

Numbers four, five and six followed as easily as the first three, and the lock popped open.

“Good job!” Jess said. “You got it to blow!”

"Poor phrasing in so many ways."

Inside the box was a brick of C4 with a digital stopwatch attached to it. The numbers on the watch read 1:34. Jake watched in mounting horror as the numbers counted down to 1:33, then 1:32.

"Uh, Jess? There *is* a timer on this detonator."

"What? Scan the bomb again."

Jake obliged, and Jess said, "Holy shit. Okay, um... What color wires do you have?"

"All black."

"Of course. Okay, you want the second row of wires deep, the third one from farthest from you."

"What?"

"I don't know how else to explain it. There should be two rows of wires. You want the one that's deeper into the bomb. Then look at the 'top' of that row and count three down."

"Three down or two down?"

"Oh Jesus, Jake. One, two, three."

"All right. Stay calm, Jess. There's nothing different about this than the bomb in the White House. We just happen to be in a White House that flies."

"Not helpful."

"All right, well, I've got the wire. What do I do now?"

"Hold that carefully and cut every other wire."

There were few things Jess could have said to make Jake nervous. That was one of them. "Cut every other wire?"

"Yes. Without pulling that wire out of its connector."

Jake looked down at the wire, which was already stretched taut in between his fingers. "This is like the kill-switch or something?"

"Sure, whatever you want to call it. Just leave it intact and cut the rest of the wires. Maybe do it now since we have what, twenty seconds left?"

They actually had eleven.

"Oh, Goddammit."

Jake pulled his multitool out and quickly opened it with one hand. He selected the wire cutters and quickly began. He had eight wires to cut, and he had only nine seconds left when he started.

"Come on, come on, come on, come on, come on."

He finally snapped the last wire just as the timer hit zero. For a terrifying split second, he waited for the world to turn white.

Then, the timer reset to five minutes.

He breathed a sigh of relief. "Okay, Jess. I—"

4:59… 4:58…

"Oh, for crying out loud."

"What? What is it?"

"It's counting down from five minutes now."

"Again? What the hell is that thing?"

"A pain in my ass is what it is. Any ideas now?"

"Um… Um… Okay, wave the scanning tool over it again."

It was a testament to Jess's anxiety that she called the tool by its actual name and not "wand thingy." Jake waved the tool over it, and Jess cursed softly.

"Shit?" Jake said. "No, I don't like that word. Please tell me you have another one."

"I have a lot of other ones," she said. "They all mean the same thing. There's no way to stop that timer without breaking it, and doing that detonates the bomb."

Jake ran his hands through his hair. "I refuse to accept that this is the end. There has to be a way to stop this."

"Unless you can figure out a way to get it off the aircraft, we're done for."

Jake cast around in his mind, desperate for an idea. Then one came to him. He looked at the straps holding the box to the hold. "If I cut the straps to the box, will it detonate?"

"No, but…" She paused briefly, and then both of them said it together. "If you get it to a door, you can throw it outside."

"Exactly. I'm going to cut the straps. Call the cockpit and have him tell our escorts to climb above us and well out of our way. I don't know how far this explosion will carry at altitude, but I don't want to be the only guy to shoot down an F-22."

"F-35."

"What?"

"They're F-35s now. The F-22s had to land, remember?"

"I… sure, fine. Three minutes left, Jess, let's focus."

"You're the one talking when you should be cutting."

Jake quickly switched the multi-tool over to the saw attachment. The blade was only four inches long and in Jake's opinion more of a novelty than an actual tool. It bit reluctantly into the leather, and it took Jake two minutes to cut the strap off.

Finally, he got it loose. "Okay, Jess. Do I need to know anything special to open these doors?"

"There's an emergency door thirty yards ahead of you at the back of the hold. That one works like the emergency doors in an airliner. Lift the handle up, push it out, then toss the bomb. Please try to not also toss yourself. You're going to lose pressure very fast, too, so try not to pass out."

“I’ll do my best.”

Jake ran to the emergency door. Thirty seconds left.

He untied his belt and looped around the handrail in the hold, then around two of his belt loops. He would have to hope the fabric held.

Ten seconds.

“Here goes.”

He opened the door handle and kicked it open. Instantly, he was sucked toward the door as the pressurized air of the hold rushed from the plane. He braced himself and held tightly to his belt.

Three seconds.

He tossed the bomb and closed his eyes.

CHAPTER FIFTEEN

With the plane traveling at eighty percent of the speed of sound away from the explosion, the sound was anticlimactic, a soft crack like a pellet rifle rather than the boom Jake expected.

He heard cheering over the earpiece though. "You did it! Ha! Take that, terrorists! Okay, close the door and come on inside."

"No door!" Jake shouted, already gasping for air.

He ducked as the cargo slid across the floor of the hold toward the open door. Boxes and crates slammed into him. He covered his head with one hand and tried to hold onto his belt with his other hand, but when a large crate of food smacked into him, it pushed him out of the airplane.

Jake heard his belt loop rip and grabbed the belt with both hands. The air pressure was insane. Even in the thin upper atmosphere, it almost overwhelmed him. He gasped, but his lungs wouldn't draw in oxygen, no matter how hard he tried.

Air, air everywhere, and not a drop to breathe.

Spots formed in his vision, and Jake knew he didn't have long before he passed out. Remembering his Marine Corps training, he forced his exhales out in grunts and breathed deeply. That maximized the amount of oxygen he could extract from the air, but it wouldn't keep him conscious for long.

Using all of his strength, he pulled himself back into the airplane. With the pressurized air expelled, the pressure inside the hold was far less than outside, and after pulling himself along the rail away from the door, he was able to get to his feet and start walking toward the hatch.

There was something viscerally terrifying about being unable to breathe. Jake was not given to fear, certainly not to fear for his own life, but as each breath brought less and less oxygen and the blackness at the edges of his vision slowly extended inward, terror seized his heart. It bypassed all of his training and experience and unlocked a reaction that was more animal than human.

He gasped and scrambled for the ladder, swaying and stumbling as unconsciousness threatened. When he reached the ladder, he ran up, not paying attention to the fact that the hatch was closed. He smashed into it hard enough to break his nose and cried out as blood sprayed down his face.

"Hold on, Jake!"

He heard the voice, but he didn't register who spoke or what exactly those words meant. It wasn't until he felt strong arms dragging him through the hatch and drew in a deep, rich breath full of oxygen that his senses started to return.

"Oh, shit!" he gasped. "Damn!"

"Stay calm," Jess's voice said. "Just breathe."

The whistling noise in the cabin stopped, and Jake lifted his head to see Merrill slamming the hatch to the hold shut. Jake collapsed onto his back and found himself still struggling to breathe, though not nearly as much as before.

He recalled the reason for that a moment later. "Nose broken?"

Jess nodded. "Oh yeah. In several places."

"Lovely."

"Eh. Better than before, but it doesn't do anything to help your lantern jaw."

He rolled his eyes, and Jess giggled. Then she threw her arms around him and hugged him tightly. "I hate you," she whispered.

"Yeah, yeah." He returned her embrace and said, "Keep this one short, or I'm going to get blood all over your uniform."

"Eww." Jess stood quickly. "You're gross."

Jake laughed. The movement sent pain through his face, and he winced. "All right. Merrill, do me a favor and trade places with Patel so he can fix my nose."

"Fix might be a bit of a stretch, boss," Merrill said, "but I'll have him look at it, at least."

"Works for me."

A few minutes later, Jake rested on the couch in the main cabin while Patel carefully set the broken pieces of Jake's nose.

"This is what I get for pissing off my parents and not becoming a doctor," he said. "I've become a damned doctor."

"I'll tell everyone that Jess set my nose while you singlehandedly fought all of the terrorists at once."

"If you keep doing stupid things like this, I'll have to fight the terrorists. Hold still."

He wrenched Jake's nose back into position, and Jake cried out.

"Oh, you big baby," Patel said, "that didn't hurt."

"You want me to break your nose and then twist it?"

“I actually think I could take you right now. We’ll arrange a sparring match as soon as we’re all debriefed. With a hurt nose and recovering from oxygen deprivation, I think I have a good shot.”

“Keep thinking that. I like putting—Ow! Goddammit! Where was the warning that time?”

“That was for my own pleasure. Now, as a medic, I’m supposed to tell you to ice it and try to avoid situations where you might get hit in the nose, but I know you’d ignore me even in the best circumstances, so I’ll just tell you that I’m not interested in hearing you bitch about it.”

“Some bedside manner you have, doc.”

“I’m not into making people feel good. I’m into making people who threaten the President feel either bad or nothing at all. That’s why I’m salty about being everyone’s favorite nurse.”

“But you’re so pretty in scrubs. Ow!”

“Another one for my benefit. All right, sir. That’s the best I can do for now.”

“Thank you,” Jake said, sitting up. “Hopefully I can do the same for you one day. Really soon.”

“I’ll keep you in mind.”

Patel returned to the galley and sent Merrill back to his post, guarding the prisoners with Gutierrez. Jake smiled at Jess and said, "Good job back there."

“You’re welcome. Thanks for helping me with your wand thingy.”

Jake rolled his eyes.

His earpiece buzzed. “Jake? It’s Trent. Captain needs to talk to you.”

“On my way.”

Jake headed toward the cabin. As he did, he heard the engines quiet and felt the nose pitch down slightly. He frowned, and as soon as he was in the cabin, he said, “What’s going on? Are we all right?”

“We’re all right, but that little hole you put in our airframe necessitates that we fly lower and slower. I’m taking us down to twenty thousand feet and three hundred knots.”

“How many hours to Honolulu then?”

“Six. We can stay in the air for another three if you still want to push it to twenty-four hours.”

“No, that’s fine. The bomb’s gone. In fact, forget about Honolulu. How far is Hickam Air Force Base?”

“That’s in Honolulu too, so that’s still six hours..”

“Not less?”

"Not in this condition. You're asking a lot of the old girl."

Jake sighed, "All right, fair enough."

You want to tell our escorts the new plan?"

"Yes."

Ian hit the radio, and Jake said. "Diamond One, do you copy?"

"It's Raven One now," an unfamiliar voice said, "but yes, I can hear you. Thanks for the heads up on that Fox Three. I was about the same distance from you as the missile was when it went off."

Jake chuckled. "Well, as much as I'd love to claim my first air-to-air kill, I don't think your wingman would be very happy with me, so I'll have to wait."

Raven one laughed. "I'll make sure to pin the victory medal on you myself."

"I'll hold you to that. Anyway, I'm calling because we're changing our destination again. Sorry to keep doing this to you, but I want us on the ground as fast as possible."

"You're going to touch down at Hickam Air Force Base?"

"Yes, sir."

"I figured as much. We're going to rendezvous with a tanker in about an hour. You're welcome to take on more fuel too if you'd like."

"We'll take you up on that offer. Just in case."

"Of course. Outstanding work, by the way, Special Agent. I know you wore the wrong uniform back when you served, but I'll talk to my squadron commander. I'm pretty sure we can get you an honorary pair of Air Force wings."

Jake laughed. "I'll wear them proudly… right underneath my globe and anchor."

"Once more, the USAF has to carry the Marine Corps. I get it."

Jake laughed again. "We'll agree to disagree on that. Thank you, Raven One."

He handed the radio back to Ian. "All right, Captain. Should be smooth sailing from here on out."

"Those are famous last words, Special Agent."

"I know, but give me a few minutes of optimism before something else goes wrong, will you?"

"Of course. "Please feel free to be as optimistic as you'd like."

Jake left the cockpit and headed for the President's stateroom. He really was feeling optimistic now. He and his agents had foiled the terrorists at every turn. He had no doubt that they would continue to frustrate them. Besides, how many bombs could they have on the plane?

Well, just in case.

"Hey Jess? Could you use your wand thingy to scan the plane and see if there are any more bombs?"

"I can try. It's not really a perfect tool, though. We'd have to get lucky and get it within an inch or two of a bomb, just like we did when we disarmed the last one."

"Well, trying something is better than nothing. Give it a shot and see if you come up with anything."

"Will do."

He reached the stateroom and knocked on the door. "Roberts? It's Mercer."

Roberts opened the door. In front of the President, his professional demeanor remained impeccable, but he allowed himself to congratulate his boss. "Good job, sir."

"Thank you, Roberts. May I come in?"

That question was answered when Sheila pushed past Roberts and leapt into Jake's arms. She kissed him passionately, and this time, Jake didn't care that Carrie was watching. When Sheila pulled away, Jake noticed that the First Lady's disapproving stare seemed a little less disapproving now.

"So it's over?" she asked Jake. "We're safe now?"

"It appears that way, ma'am."

"What do you mean, it appears that way?"

"He means yes, mom," Sheila said, taking Jake's hand and leading him to the couch. "Sit down. I'm going to get you some snacks and a glass of champagne."

"I'll take the snacks, but I'll save the champagne for after this is all over."

"Oh, come on, Jake," the President said, coming out of the attached bedroom. "Indulge for a bit. You've saved all of our lives."

Jake nodded and said, "Well, if you insist, sir."

"I do in—"

Bryan didn't get a chance to finish that sentence. The plane lurched forward, and all five people in the room skidded forward and fell against the forward wall.

CHAPTER SIXTEEN

Jake put his hands and arms out in front of him and caught himself just before he slammed into the First Lady. Carrie stared up at him in shock. Her eyes narrowed, and for a moment, Jake thought she was going to hit him. "What now?" she asked.

Well, you see, ma'am, this is all going according to my diabolical plan. I just can't wait to kill you and your family, including your daughter who I love.

He controlled himself, and instead answered, "I don't know."

That probably wasn't much more helpful.

"Well, find out!"

Nope, not any more helpful at all.

Jake tapped his earpiece. "What's going on, cockpit?"

"I don't know!" Ian said, "I've lost flight controls!"

"How long until we—"

"Not long! I'm going to reboot the system!"

The next several seconds were the most terrifying of Jake's life. For Sheila's sake, he held himself together, but at any moment, he expected the plane to disintegrate as it impacted the ocean.

Then the nose began to pitch upward. The groaning of the engines and the overstressed airframe calmed. Sheila burst into tears of relief and clung to Jake while Bryan helped steady his wife as the plane righted itself.

"What was that?" he asked Jake. "Are we all right?"

"I'm going to find out. Roberts? Are you good?"

Roberts was picking himself up from a puddle of champagne and shattered glass. Fortunately, none of the glass had reached his eyes.

"I'm all right, sir. I'll keep an eye on things here."

"All right. For the moment, I want you and your family seated and buckled in, Mr. President. I'm going to go to the cockpit and figure out what happened."

"Understood. Be careful, Jake."

"I love you," Sheila added.

Carrie sighed loudly.

At least she didn't threaten to kill me this time.

Jake left the stateroom and tapped his earpiece. “Team, check in. How are we doing?”

“I’m good,” Jess said. “I managed to save my laptop too.”

“Good. Try to figure out what happened.”

“No, really?”

“Not now, Jess.”

Patel was next. “Galley is good, sir. Chef’s pissed off about the sauce we spilled, but there are no injuries.”

“Can’t say the same for the prisoners,” Merrill said. “Franz hit his head and knocked himself out. He’s still alive, though.”

“Too bad. Maybe we’ll get him next time.”

“Okay, seriously?” Jess chimed in. “After giving me crap about my humor?”

“I’ll buy you a hoagie when we get home. Cockpit?”

“You might want to come down here, sir.”

“Already here.”

Trent opened the door, and Jake stepped into the cockpit. “What’s going on? What happened?”

He looked around the cockpit and saw that all the lights and screens were off. “What’s going on?”

Ian gripped the yoke tightly and held the throttle with the other hand. “I’m on backup instruments for everything now. And I mean everything. The autopilot tried to make us crash.”

Jake sighed. “Another sabotage.”

It wasn’t a question.

“I guess so,” Ian replied. “All I know is that the only way to keep us airborne right now is to fly this thing like it’s the nineteen-twenties. I tried rebooting the system, and it wouldn’t reset. I tried shutting the autopilot off, and it refused. I had to pull the emergency shutdown switch and cut off all electronic power. I don’t even have FADEC of fly-by-wire anymore.”

“That means no computer assistance to fly?”

“None. No maintaining airspeed or attitude without constant input from me.”

“Jesus. No radio either?”

“No.”

“All right. Keep heading toward Hawaii. I’m going to go talk to Jess and see if she can help.”

Jake made his way back to the main cabin. Jess sported a fresh bruise on her forehead, and the table was covered with the remains of her coffee. “Hey, tiger,” she said halfheartedly when he approached. “What’s cookin’, toots?”

“Can you get me radio? I need to talk to the escorts.”

“Yeah, I can do that. Give me one second.”

A moment later, Jake heard the panicked voice of the lead escort. “Air Force One, this is Raven One! Acknowledge!”

“Raven One, this is Air Force One. We experienced a serious systems failure, and we were forced to shut down the computer. We’re currently flying on analog instruments only. My understanding is that there’s no digital assistance for any aircraft systems. Captain Sontag is currently flying by hand.”

After a brief pause, Raven One said, “Okay, Air Force One. Please advise what you’d like to do.”

“Can you refuel and catch up to us if we keep heading straight for Hickam?”

“I can do you one better. I’ll contact the tanker and have him match your speed and heading.”

“Perfect. That’s still the plan. We’ll just have to do it the old-fashioned way. Make contact with Hickam if you haven’t already and have emergency crews ready as soon as we land. Transport too. I want the President to be able to take off ASAP and head home. Make sure it’s in a plane that can’t possibly have been tampered with.”

“I’ll do my best for all of that, sir.”

“Your best has to include everything that I just mentioned, Raven One. I’m sorry to be harsh, but this is the President.” For a little extra motivation, he added, “Time to show me how badass you Air Force boys are.”

“You had to go there,” Raven One said, “All right. One proof positive, coming right up.”

The slightly more relaxed tone of the escort calmed Jake a little after their latest brush with death.

Whatcha got for me now, Trident? You’re batting zero.

“Okay, Jess. I need you to keep monitoring this channel. Right now, you’re our only connection with our escorts, or hell, with anybody. Not to pile on once more, but any information you can give me about how our systems were compromised like that would be awesome as well.”

“You got it, chocolate chip.”

“I don’t think that works, but if it makes you feel better.”

“It does, so shut up and leave me alone.”

Jake headed for the prisoners' cabin next. Merrill opened to reveal an even angrier Gutierrez glaring down at a chuckling Dana Porter.

Dana turned to Jake when he entered and said, "Special Agent Mercer, we have a problem here. You're agent here says that he doesn't like rollercoasters."

"Why isn't she gagged?" Jake asked.

"We took it off," Merrill informed him. "We were trying to get her to tell us what just happened."

"Excellent idea," Jake said. "And what did she say?"

"I said I felt bad that your men were such cowards. It must be hard to see a bunch of terrorists braver than you are."

Jake pulled his knife from its scabbard and pressed the tip against a point just behind Dana's jaw. The terrorist kept her defiant attitude, but Jake felt her stiffen slightly.

"I'm not in the mood, Dana," he said. "Tell me what happened and how to stop it, or I'll give you a new grin to laugh out of."

"My my. We lose our self-control so quickly when—"

Jake began to slice forward, and Dana cried out, "All right! All right!"

Jake removed the knife, and a trickle of blood ran down her cheek. The other terrorists watched with huge eyes. "That's right," Jake said, looking at Dana but talking to all of them. "This is Air Force One. We're the Secret Service, and the only rights you have here are to do exactly as I say when I say it. You want to lecture someone about how immoral that is, save it for your buddies in prison."

"We have friends too, Mercer," Dana said, shaking with fear and rage. "That's what happened to your damned plane. But once more, you assholes found a way to get around that Why the hell won't you just fucking die?"

"Wouldn't that be so much easier?" Jake said. "By the way, why *aren't* we dead? I notice that your buddy Fritz here managed to incapacitate three of my agents but didn't think to make that incapacitation permanent. I think you're not telling me the whole truth."

"Screw you!"

Jake knelt in front of Dana and waved the knife in front of her. "Last chance before I make an example of you and move on to one of your buddies."

Dana's defiant look faltered, and she swallowed anxiously. She looked at her friends, but they were all gagged and could do little more than stare. Jake turned toward those stares. Coulson kept his eyes on the floor, not daring to look up at what was happening. Franz was still groggy from hitting his head and only managed to blink and stare somewhat confusedly.

Melina stared hard at Dana, her eyes boring into the relief captain with far more strength than she had shown before, even when she was first caught. Maybe Dana wasn't the leader after all.

Jake stood. "Gag her."

Gutierrez obliged, and Jake walked to Coulson. He tore the tape off of the disgraced agent's mouth and said, "Okay, buddy. Time to do the right thing. Tell me what happened."

Coulson shook his head. "I don't know. I really don't know. I was hired to plant the bomb. They didn't tell me anything else."

Jake put the tip of the knife under Coulson's chin and started to lift it. Coulson yanked his head angrily away and said, "Look, kill me if you want, Jake. I did what I was told to do. You already know my reasons. I don't know anything else."

"Who's in charge?"

Coulson frowned, but his eyes flicked to Melina.

"Thank you. Gag him again."

Jake dragged Melina to the back room where he had interrogated Dana and Coulson and set her on the bunk. Unlike with them, he left her bound and only tore off the gag. She grimaced and glared at him, then chuckled. "My my, Jake. We like it rough, don't we?"

"Like I told your friends, I'm not in the mood."

"It's all right. You can be rough with me. I won't bite. Unless you ask me to."

Jake put his knife away, and Melina laughed again. "Ooh. What are you gonna—"

Jake slapped her hard enough to knock her from the bunk onto the floor. She gasped and shuddered, mouth open in shock from the pain.

"I told you, I'm not in the mood. How are you controlling Air Force One?"

"We have friends," she gasped. "Dana already told you."

"Who are your friends?"

"Fellow patriots."

Jake lifted his hand, and she growled. "Fuck you. Do whatever you want to me. I made my peace with it."

Jake lowered his hand and drew his knife again.

"Kill me!" she hissed. "Kill me, you coward!"

Jake knelt in front of her and swung the knife tip lazily in front of Melina's eyes.

Melina swallowed, unable to hide her anxiety. Jake wasn't actually going to torture her for information, but if he could convince her that he really *was* that brutal, then maybe she would tell him what he needed to know. He was running out of options at this point.

"Jake," Jess called over his earpiece. "I need you."

Jess's tone was tense and frightened. Jake sighed and stood, "It's your lucky day."

He sheathed his knife and grabbed Melina, yanking her to her feet. He dropped her off in the prisoners' room and headed to the main cabin.

"What is it?"

"The malfunction was caused by another EM pulse."

"Another one? From where?"

Jess met his eyes. "From above us. A satellite."

CHAPTER SEVENTEEN

Jake stared at Jess in shock. “A satellite?”

“Unless you know of another way we could have been hit by an EM pulse from three hundred thirty miles above us.”

Jake ran his hands through his head. “The plot thickens. Any idea what satellite?”

“No. None.”

“Can you find out?”

“I can give you a rough guess.” She pulled up a map of the U.S. satellite constellation. “We have two GPS satellites, a defense satellite, and seven spy satellites.”

“How can ten satellites be three hundred thirty miles away?”

“That was a rough guess. There are ten satellites within five hundred miles that could have placed a signal on us. Those are just U.S. satellites. If we expand it to include all nations…” she typed a command into her laptop. “We’re looking at eight more satellites.”

“Jesus. And there’s no way you can trace the signal to its exact location?”

“I can, but it’s incredibly risky.”

“How so?”

That EM pulse was powerful enough to short out an aircraft carrier. It’ll melt my laptop if whoever fired it figures out that I’m looking.”

“If it’s powerful enough to short out an aircraft carrier, then why didn’t it short out Air Force One? Why did it just cause the systems to go haywire?”

“The systems went haywire because they were shorted out. The primary fuse boxes are all toast, and the surge was powerful enough to destroy our external digital sensors. So when the secondary boxes came online, the information they were receiving was all inaccurate. Air Force One thought it was leveling out from a steep climb when it was really pushing us into a steep dive.”

Jake sighed and sat next to Jess. He suddenly felt very tired. “Call Raven One for me.”

Jess did so, and Jake said, “Raven One, it’s Air Force One.”

“Roger Air Force One. I’d ask for good news, but it doesn’t seem to be our day.”

“No, sir, it doesn’t. We figured out what happened to our controls.”

“What’s that?”

“A cyber attack from one of… well, we’re not sure if it’s one of our satellites, but it’s *a* satellite. I suspect one of ours because that’s what…” he stopped himself. He didn’t have time to explain all about Trident, so he only said, “that’s what we think our terrorists would have had access to.”

“A cyber attack from a satellite? Like a carrier wave?”

“No, like an EM pulse.”

“Can’t be an EM pulse. That would have fried us and the tanker too. We’re only a hundred yards ahead of you, and the tanker is only fifty yards in front of us.”

“Well, it shorted out our primary fuse box and fused some of our sensors together.”

“You mean the sensor wiring, but I get your point. Okay, for the signal to be that precise, it would have to be a military satellite. For it to be that powerful, it would have to be a defense satellite. I’m not familiar with where those are located, but that’s what I’d be looking for.”

“That’s helpful, thank you.”

“Well, I don’t know if helpful is the right word. If a defense satellite targeted you, it can target you again. Are you using aircraft systems to communicate?”

“No, we’re on a private connection.”

“Is your antenna inside or outside the aircraft?”

“Inside.”

“Okay, that’s good. Disconnect it from any power sources attached to the airplane. It’s damned miraculous the surge didn’t already short it out, but the next one probably will.”

Jess unplugged her laptop, and Jake said, “Okay, that’s done.”

“All right. Here’s the next problem. If they aim at us, there’s no chance in hell we survive it. We’re going to switch to piggyback link. I’m going to make my aircraft the primary communications node and get us off satellite. Raven Two, Oasis Three, prepare to transfer your systems to me on my mark. Air Force One, we’ll lose you for about fifteen seconds while that happens, then I’ll send you a signal to reconnect.”

“Understood, Raven One.”

The channel cut off, and Jake said, "Damn. Those new stealth fighters are badass."

"God bless the USA."

"How long can your laptop run on battery power?"

"With all the work it's doing? About eight hours."

"Okay. That's only an hour less than our twenty-four hour cutoff anyway. We'll have to make do."

"Hold on," Jess said. "That's Raven One."

She pressed a key on her laptop. "Go ahead, Raven One."

"Wonderful. Okay, so we have communications, but we don't have GPS navigation. In a few years, we're supposed to get a backup GPS receiver, but that doesn't help us now. What we *do* have is terrain-mapping radar and the excellent training of the most outstanding of the nation's military branches."

Jake chuckled. "You have me at a disadvantage, Captain, so I have no choice but to accept your statement."

Raven One laughed. "Hey, if it makes you feel better, I don't think I could have tossed a bomb out of a cargo hold and then crawled my way back to safety, so I guess we all have our place in the wheel of American badassery."

"I'll take it."

"The point of all this is I can guide you to Hickam and help you land. So fuck terrorists, and I hope they watch in impotent rage as we lift a collective middle finger to them."

"Ooh, rah."

"Can you patch me through to your cockpit?"

"Sure can. Captain Sontag, do you read?"

"I read you loud and clear, Jake."

"All right. Raven One's going to be our new navigator. He's going to walk you through what you need to do, so just follow his instructions."

"Yes, sir."

"Perfect. Quick question, Raven One: could our defense satellite send another power surge to destroy your systems?"

"Maybe, but it would be a lot harder. I'll save you the technical mumbo-jumbo and just tell you that it's extremely hard to find us, even when we're using radar. We shift radar wavelengths somewhere in the neighborhood of a billion times a second. That's probably an exaggeration, but you get where I'm going with this."

"And they didn't want to do that for Air Force One?"

"From my understanding, the new VC-25Bs will have this technology. Thank the budgeteers in Congress for dragging their feet with the program."

"I'm sure the President will have many words of thanks for them," Jake replied. "All right. Looks like we've found another light at the end of yet another tunnel. Knock on wood this is the last emergency we have to solve."

"Your mouth to God's ears."

"Amen. Raven One out."

Jake sighed and rubbed his eyes. "I have to hand it to Bard. He really pulled all the stops out on this one."

Jess would normally follow that up with something witty, but instead, she cupped her chin with her thumb and forefinger and bit her lip.

Jake didn't like that look. "What now?"

"Well, that defense satellite is part of the new PULSAR network."

"What's PULSAR?"

"Think STAR WARS but closer to the actual sci-fi franchise than the Reagan-era spy network."

"What does that mean?"

"It means that if they get really desperate, they might be able to use a directed energy beam to quite literally blow us out of the sky."

Jake's shoulders slumped. "A laser beam?"

"I'm told that's an amateurish way to describe it. But yes."

"Oh my God." Jake leaned back and lifted his hands in mock supplication. "Really? Laser weapons? I shudder to ask what's next."

"I need to call someone," Jess said. "Someone back in Washington. We need that satellite shut down. Hell, we need all of them shut down."

Jake tapped his earpiece. "Raven One, we've identified the satellite used."

There was a brief pause, then a youthful voice replied, "Air Force One, this is Raven Two. Raven One is occupied with navigating for all four birds right now, so I'll be your liaison."

"Okay, Raven Two. We need to make contact with NORAD or the Pentagon, ASAP. Those satellites can shoot us out of the sky."

There was another brief pause. "Okay. Um… Let me talk to Raven One."

The channel cut off for a moment. Then Raven One came online. "Air Force One, I've been apprised of the situation. Can you confirm that it's PULSAR that fired that EM pulse?"

"Yes, Raven One. It's the only defense satellite in range that could do the job."

"All right. This is what we're going to do. Raven Two is going to break off and fly perpendicular to our route. When he's thirteen miles away, he's going to reactivate his GPS and send your message to NORAD. They'll be able to shut down PULSAR until the sabotage can be figured out. Then he's going to come back to us. That process will take about fifteen minutes to complete."

Jake and Jess shared a look. Fifteen minutes was an eternity.

"While this is taking place, Oasis Three will adjust its transponder signal to mimic Air Force One's and fly in the opposite direction of Raven Two. If PULSAR tries to shoot, the hope is that they'll shoot the tanker and not Air Force One."

"There's no other way?" Jess asked.

"No good way. I'm going to clear the channel for now, and I'll ask for you to do the same until this gets worked out. Don't worry about us, ma'am. I speak for every member of the Air Force when I say it's a privilege to put our lives on the line to defend our President."

"Well, Jake's a personal friend of the President, and I'm a personal friend of Jake's. I'll make sure you all get medals for this."

Raven One chuckled. "That's kind of you, ma'am, but I'd rather hear Jake say out loud that the Air Force is better than the Marine Corps."

Jake laughed and shook his head. "I'd just like it on record that this is occurring under duress and does not reflect my true beliefs nor does it reflect reality."

"Whatever you need to tell yourself, jarhead. Raven One out."

The channel cut off, and Jake met Jess's eyes. "I like him."

"Me too. I wonder if he's single?"

"When we're all safe on the ground, I'll ask him for you."

"I can ask him myself, thank you very much."

The two of them fell silent, and their smiles quickly faded. Jake looked out the window at the pitch-black sky. He prayed that the darkness wouldn't be interrupted by the sight of the tanker exploding. Too many innocent people had died at Trident's hands.

You'll get yours, Bard, he promised silently. *You'll pay for every single one of those deaths.*

CHAPTER EIGHTEEN

Jake knocked on the door to the President's stateroom. Instead of Roberts' voice, he heard the first lady cry out, "No! I'm sick of him interrupting us every ten damned minutes! He needs to do his job and get us down!"

Jake lowered his head. He didn't have the energy to feel angry anymore. Besides, her fear was understandable, even if it was misplaced. Sheila herself sometimes redirected her fear into anger at her father for choosing a career that put them in this kind of danger.

Roberts spoke into his mouthpiece. His tone was formal, but Jake could hear the irritation behind it. "The First Lady has requested privacy, Special Agent Mercer. Is this update critical?"

"No, Roberts. I have an update on our situation, but it doesn't require action from the President or his family. I'll leave them alone."

"Hold on," the President's voice said. "I'll talk to him outside."

"Is that all right with you, sir?" Roberts asked Jake.

"Yeah, it's fine. The prisoners are secure, and for the moment, Air Force One is safe from attack."

That wasn't true, but if they were struck by a satellite laser, it wouldn't really matter where the President was.

"All right, sir. Shall I accompany the President or stay with his family?"

"Stay with his family. Thank you, Roberts."

"Of course, sir."

The door opened, and Bryan came out. He smiled at Jake, but Jake could see his exhaustion in the stoop of his shoulders and the bags under his eyes. "Hey, Jake. More good news?"

"Well, more news, sir. We've discovered the source of the most recent attack. It appears that one of our PULSAR satellites has been compromised. They fired an EM pulse at Air Force One and shorted out our systems. The autopilot attempted to fly us into the ocean. That's what happened an hour ago. We were able to recover when Captain Sontag disabled the computer. He's now flying using piggyback navigation from one of our escorts."

"Got it. Gotta love those new stealth fighters, huh?"

"They're damned impressive sir. So the plan now is to have NORAD disable the satellite. They can't damage us with another EM pulse since we have the digital systems shut off, but they can—"

A light flashed from behind them, and Jake's face fell.

"What was that?" Bryan asked.

The answer was exactly what Jake feared it would be.

"Jake…" Jess said softly. "PULSAR shot down Oasis Three."

Jake's shoulders slumped. "Understood, Jess."

"Air Force One, this is Raven One." The Air Force Captain's voice was somber, but he held his composure well. "As you probably already know, PULSAR has shot down Oasis Three, believing it to be Air Force One. I have the crew manifest on board, so I'll make sure that they're remembered for their heroism. The good news is that Raven Two just reported that NORAD received their message. He'll keep his distance until we get confirmation that PULSAR is shut down, but it looks like we've managed to keep the President safe."

"Thank you, Raven One. I wish I could think of something to say to express our gratitude."

The President's brow furrowed. "Jake? What happened?"

Jake sighed. "We used a tanker as a decoy Air Force One to throw PULSAR off the scent so they didn't shoot us down. The decoy appears to have worked as intended, sir."

The President seemed to deflate right in front of Jake. Jake had seen the President's human side more than most, but seeing him not as the Commander-in-Chief, but as an old, tired man was perhaps the most sobering thing Jake had experienced throughout this ordeal.

"Thank you, Jake," he said softly. "May I speak with our escort?"

Jake nodded and handed Bryan his earpiece. Bryan took a deep breath, then straightened his shoulders and affected the air of quiet command Jake had grown accustomed to seeing from him. "Sir? This is the President speaking." After a pause, the President said, "I want to thank you and your officers for the efforts you've all put into keeping me and my family safe. There's nothing I can say that will mitigate the loss of those men and women aboard the tanker. All I can say is that they will be honored for their sacrifice. So will you, and so will your wingman. Thank you."

He handed the earpiece back to Jake and smiled wanly. "I'm going to go back to my family now. Do me a favor and don't tell Sheila. She's having a hard enough time with everything as it is."

"I won't, sir," Jake promised.

Bryan nodded and managed another smile. "Thank you, Jake. You'll be honored for your service as well."

"That's not why I'm here, sir."

"I know. But you'll be honored anyway. It's important that heroes are remembered, even if they don't want to be. The nation is…" he shook his head. "Well, we're not used to this kind of adversity. People are afraid, and they have a right to be. The best thing we can do is give them people to look up to. America only falls when we allow fear to rule us. That's not a campaign speech, and it's not a political statement. It's the truth. So you'll be receiving a medal for this, not for you, but for America. Perhaps the hardest thing I'll ever have to ask of you is that you wear it with pride whether you want to or not."

That is not even remotely the hardest thing you've asked of me, sir, Jake didn't say. Aloud, he only said, "I will, sir."

"Good." Bryan clapped Jake on the shoulder, smiled again, then headed into his room.

Jake stood where he was for a while, head bowed. He felt so tired. Maybe that was Trident's plan. Wear him down—wear everyone down until all anyone could do was give up and let him do whatever he wanted to do.

His exhaustion slowly gave way to anger and contempt. What a small man Bard was. What a small, insecure little man to kill and terrorize others to inflate his own self-worth.

There's a special place in Hell for you, Bard, he thought, *but I'm not going to leave much for the Devil to play with.*

"Air Force One, this is Raven One."

Jake took a breath and squared his shoulders. "Go ahead, Raven One."

"Just wanted to let you know we're all set. PULSAR is down. Raven Two and I are back on satellite link. We called Hickam, and they're sending us another tanker. We'll reach Hickam in four hours."

"Thank you, Raven One."

"Of course. As I said earlier, sir, it's an honor. We all knew the job when we signed up. Besides, we can't let you jarheads be the only martyrs."

Jake could only manage a half-smile at that.

"Yeah," Raven One said. "That didn't make me feel better either."

"Let's get this bird on the ground," Jake said. "That'll make me feel better."

"Hell yeah. That's Air Force for ooh rah, by the way."

Jake chuckled at that one. "Ooh rah, Raven One."

Jake returned to the main cabin and sat down next to Jess. Jess's eyes were red and puffy, and her lips trembled slightly as she smiled at Jake. "Hey, buddy."

Jake acted impulsively, pulling Jess into his arms and embracing her tightly. Jess stiffened for a moment, then relaxed, gripping his shoulders tightly and shaking softly with the force of her sobs. They held each other for a long moment, silently comforting each other for everything they'd had to endure, everything they'd had to watch others endure. Faces flashed in Jake's mind of people who had lost their lives in the fight against Trident from the first Lincoln Memorial attack through today.

So many dead. So many lives hurt to appease the ego of one insane man.

Finally, Jess pulled away. She sighed and said, "My compliments to Sheila. Whatever cologne she's having you where is perfect."

Jake chuckled. "I'll be sure to tell her that."

"Ah," Jess said, taking her seat again. "If I ever see Bard face to face, I'm going to plug a car battery into him and rev the engine until he crumbles into dust."

"You'll have to get in line. On a serious note, if Bard or Bard's contact could get to PULSAR, it's a good bet he can get into other things. How many people even have access to those satellites?"

"They're NORAD satellites, so that would be NORAD, obviously, or USNORTHCOM. Possibly USPACOM. Other than that, I couldn't tell you."

"But NORAD is most likely."

"Yes. And I don't know how their systems work, so I don't know if a button-pusher could have done it, or if you'd need someone with command authority."

"Well, the larger issue is that if someone *does* have command authority, or the ability to push the right buttons, then we have ballistic missile submarines, missile defense systems and who knows what else they can throw at us?"

"Ballistic missiles can't hit moving targets, but I get your point. I'd like to say that now that NORAD and the Air Force are aware of the situation, we won't have trouble from NORAD anymore, but I'd also like to say that Oasis Three didn't just get shot down by a laser, so what I'd like isn't worth much, it seems."

“I need you to look into NORAD," Jake said. "You can plug your laptop back in, and you can connect to satellite communication, so reach out to your contacts in Washington and see if you can get any intel. I know that we’re focused on the immediate situation, but someone who can commandeer defense satellites is going to be the number one priority once the President is safe. Since there’s not much else to do but follow Raven One’s lead to Hickam, I want you to get a jump on that process.”

“You got it, boss.”

Jake nodded and clapped Jess’s shoulder. “Hang in there, Jess. We’re almost out of the woods.”

“I know. But what woods do we enter next?” She sighed and ran her hands through her hair. “I just want this to be over. I want Bard to die. I don’t even hate him anymore. I just want him gone so we can relax.”

“I know what you mean,” Jake said. *Can’t say I don’t hate him, though.*

He left Jake and headed for the relief cabin. Throughout this ordeal, he hadn’t taken any time for himself. He didn’t resent that, of course. Like Raven One, he had accepted every aspect of his job, even the unpleasant ones. But after watching Bard shoot a plane down just for looking like Air Force One on radar, Jake needed a moment to recover.

He sat in the jumpseat with a heavy sigh and leaned his head back. He stared up at the ceiling, not closing his eyes for fear he would fall asleep if he did that.

The three remaining engines of Air Force One hummed powerfully. The noise was almost soothing. It was as though everything was normal.

He chuckled. What the hell even was normal anymore? After the year he’d had, he wouldn’t recognize it anymore.

He used to think he would end up like his friend Max when he retired, able to put the past behind him and enjoy a successful second life in some rewarding private career. Now, he feared he would end up more like Drew. Not a terrorist, of course, but destroyed mentally and emotionally by his experiences and unable to keep from looking around every corner waiting for the next threat.

In a way, Bard had already won. He would be wiped from existence eventually, but the memory of his terror would linger in the hearts and minds of the nation he had terrorized, an ache that could fade but never disappear entirely.

Could Jake ever recover from that? Could he allow himself a normal life knowing that the terrorist he had failed to catch for months had left such a deep scar on the nation he was supposed to help protect?

Sheila dreamed of a quiet life somewhere in a quiet part of the country where they could live peacefully and act as though there was no such thing as Bard or Trident or terrorists or death.

But Jake would always know. Those memories would haunt him for the rest of his life. Could he really enjoy a peaceful retirement knowing that others were fighting and dying while he was wasting his days fishing off of his back porch?

And if he couldn't, could Sheila accept someone who would never stop fighting?

CHAPTER NINETEEN

"Jake!"

Jake opened his eyes with a sharp intake of breath and realized to his horror that he had fallen asleep after all.

"Shit."

He got up and tapped his earpiece, jogging for the main cabin. "What is it, Jess?"

"We're being attacked again."

Any semblance of exhaustion vanished when Jake heard that. "Source?"

"Working on it. It's another cyber-attack. This one's coming directly for my laptop, though."

"Your laptop?"

"Yes. Raven One confirmed they read no anomalies on their end. I'm the only one being targeted."

"Can you reboot your laptop and cut off the attack?"

"I can try."

She tapped a flurry of commands into her screen, then cursed. "They're preventing shutdown. Let me try a hard reboot."

She held down the button, and after three seconds, the screen went black. Jess sighed with relief. "Okay, we know I can turn it off. Let's see if I can turn it back on."

She pressed the power button again, and the screen brightened as the computer booted up."

"Wonderful," Jake said. "All right. That's some good news."

"Well, let's not hold our judgment. I don't know if that fixed anything yet."

"Fair enough."

The screen showed a loading screen for the BIOS, then one for the operating system, then finally one for the CIA-encrypted desktop. Jess entered her password and checked a few things. "Okay. That all looks good. Communications, check; sensors, check; bunch of cool toys that would take too long to name, check, check, check and check. Also check. Okay, looks like that did—hold on."

Jake's heart sank. "What is it?"

“Dammit, the signal’s back.”

“It’s jamming you?”

“No, it’s trying to execute commands. My firewall’s holding it off for now, but…” her fingers flew over the keys, and Jake said, “Is everything okay?”

“It’s overpowering my firewall. I’m reprogramming it, but the signal looks like it’s reprogramming itself each time I reprogram it.”

“Where is it coming from?”

“I don’t know yet. I’m using all my CPU power to keep it from overriding me.”

“And nothing from Raven One or Raven Two yet?”

“Not that I know of.”

Jake tapped his earpiece. “Raven One, do you copy?”

“We copy, Air Force One. Go ahead.”

“Can you tell what’s attacking us right now? Looks like some sort of phishing signal.”

“Loger,” Jess corrected.

"Okay, Jess says it's a longer."

“Yeah, that’s a password-cracking virus, basically. Someone’s trying to access her laptop. Have you tried rebooting it?”

“Tried that, didn’t work.”

“Okay. Well, it won’t be able to get through to us via a communication channel, but if they’re successful in logging in, they’ll be able to hear us. Please let us know if that happens. Do you have anything on that laptop that could be used to seize control of Air Force One?”

“No, but if they can mine data from my laptop, they’ll know exactly what the state of Air Force One is and what our plans are.”

“I’ll call Hickam and make sure they're on full alert. They know we're coming, so they should be prepared for any threats on the ground. We only have three hours to go, so we just need to hold out that long. If none of your equipment is flight-critical, then you can shut your laptop off if needed. I'll talk to your pilot and tell him how we can use my and my escort's aircraft lighting to guide him to landing. Don't worry, Special Agent. We've still got this under control."

“Thank you, Raven One.”

“Of course. Hang in there. It’s two minutes left in the fourth [illegible]d the other team is desperate. This is when they try all the [illegible] only works if the defense isn’t prepared.”

Jess chuckled. "I don't think I understand your analogy, but thank you."

"Still no idea where the source is?" Jake asked.

"No, I think…" her face fell. "Come on."

"What? What is it?"

"It's here. On board. The source is from the aircraft."

Jake sighed. "All right, so we're going to have to disable another terrorist device. Same bat time, same bat channel."

"The signature is weird, though. It's almost like a personal computer, just a lot more robust. Hold on, I think I've figured it out. It's generating random code, but the code is organized in a recognizable repeating pattern. Give me a minute, I think I can stop it."

She tapped more commands into her computer, and a moment later, she said, "Got it. It was the Fibonacci sequence."

"The what?"

The Fibonacci sequence. For every two numbers in the sequence, the third equals their sum. Or difference if you count from largest to smallest number. The emitter generates random binary code representing three numbers in the Fibonacci sequence in either ascending or descending order. And now"—she pressed a button—"my computer is isolating and removing every string of code that contains a Fibonacci sequence."

"Damn. Badass."

"Very much. *And*, I've captured an image of the signal, and I can trace it's origin. And it is coming from… it looks like our lockers."

"*Our* lockers?"

"Well, not ours specifically, but one of the Secret Service lockers. Maybe ours. The point is, we're out of danger, and we know where to look now."

"How would they have gotten access to our lockers?"

"How would they have been able to sneak multiple bombs on Air Force One?"

Jake shook his head. "I get your point, but those are real questions that we need real answers to. They couldn't have just sneaked all of this onto the most secure aircraft on Earth. They would have needed help, not just from Dalton."

"I agree that we need to answer that question, but let's focus on getting the plane down first. We can figure out the how and why after the President is safe."

"Fair enough. Keep your eyes and ears open, both biological and electronic, and I'll see what I can find from the lockers."

The secret service lockers were located in the three cabins that would have served as their quarters had the flight gone as planned. As Jake passed through the first cabin where the prisoners were being held, Merrill asked, "What's going on now?"

"something's trying to attack Jess's computer again."

"Seriously?"

"Yeah. Looks like something low-powered, probably a last-ditch Hail-Mary in case plans A through Q failed. Jess has it under control, but I'm going to find the source and disable it just in case."

Gutierrez chuckled and looked down at the prisoners. "Damn. I'll give you guys some credit. You tried your best. That's crazy that you did all of that just to kill the President."

"They played a good game," Jake said. "We played a better one."

He walked to the rearmost cabin. He would start there and work his way forward.

The lockers here were for Special Agents Gutierrez and Coulson, the two most junior agents. Jake expected the device—whatever it was—to be in Coulson's locker, so when he found nothing other than clothing, he was surprised.

Well, give Coulson a little credit. He probably had just enough intelligence to know not to stash a sabotaging device in his own locker.

He searched Gutierrez's things, and other than finding a contraband magazine, there was nothing there either.

He decided to let the magazine go. Not that he wouldn't tease Gutierrez about it later.

He checked the cabin itself thoroughly just in case. There was nothing there. The room was as clean as possible.

One down, two to go. He tapped his earpiece. "Hey, Jess. How are you doing?"

"I'm great! How are you?"

He rolled his eyes. "I mean, are you still able to resist the jamming signal?"

"Oh. Here I thought you actually gave a crap about me. My bad."

Jake rubbed his temples. "Jess…"

"Okay, fine. Jeez, can you not tell from my cheery attitude? Everything's good. The signal is still trying it's thing, but I've created a subroutine to make the signal think it's succeeding so I can analyze it."

"Is it telling you anything?"

“Well, it’s broadcasting on a frequency of eight hundred kilohertz. That’s within the AM radio band.”

“Is it saying anything?”

“No, just white noise. It’s a rather weak attempt to attack us, to be honest. I don’t get why they thought it would work.”

Jake frowned. “It could be a distraction. Keep an eye on it and see if you can detect anything else. They might just be trying to move our eyes away from the real plan.”

“I’ll keep an eye out. Everything looks good so far, but I’ll monitor the situation.”

“You got it. Thank you.”

He moved to the second room. This was the largest of the three cabins and contained room for four people. Merrill, Trent, Roberts, and Patel had their lockers in this room. The last place to check would be his and Jess's lockers in the first cabin where the prisoners were held. He considered having Merrill and Gutierrez look through their lockers but decided against it. The prisoners were bound tightly, but he didn't want to take any chances. He wanted eyes on them at all times.

He started with Roberts locker. Roberts was probably the most by-the-book of all the agents, and his locker showed that. He had nothing in there but the standard-issue spare uniform, a spare earpiece, and a pair of sunglasses. Jake lifted the earpiece and scanned it with the scanning tool. The “wand thingy.”

He chuckled at himself and shook his head. Wand thingy. He deserved whatever grief Jess ended up giving him for that.

The wand thingy flashed red over the earpiece as Jake turned it in his hand. From what Jess had told him, it would turn a solid green if nothing out of the ordinary was found and strobe blue if something unusual was detected.

It took about five seconds for the scanning tool to display a solid green light. Roberts’ earpiece was clean.

Patel’s locker was the most “normal” looking. It contained a uniform, a casual outfit, a pair of sweatpants, two t-shirts, and an unusual amount of personal grooming tools. Patel evidently took his appearance very seriously. Not as embarrassing as Gutierrez’s magazine, but worth some ribbing.

Jake couldn’t wait to get to the point where he would have time and energy to joke around with his agents. He just wanted this whole thing to be over. It was the first time in his career he could recall being so drained. Even when his life—and the President’s—had been in more direct danger, he couldn't remember ever being so mentally exhausted. Hell, even when he was dying of a supervirus, he couldn't remember being so overwhelmed.

"Just a few more hours," he reminded himself. "Almost there."

He checked Merrill's locker. Merrill was the most experienced of the agents, having joined the Service two months before Jake arrived. Jake wasn't surprised to discover a small radio transmitter in his locker. Whoever had planted it had done so in one of the last places Jake would think to look.

The scanning tool quickly confirmed that the transmitter was indeed the source of the jamming signal. Jake's initial plan was to disable it, but he thought again. Perhaps Jess could get some useful information out of it.

He tapped his earpiece. "Hey, Jess? I'm bringing the transmitter to you. It was in Merrill's locker. I think you should look at it before I disable it, just in case you can get something from it."

No response. Jake frowned. "Jess? Jess, are you there?"

No answer.

A chill ran through Jake's spine. He stood, preparing to run quickly to check on Jess.

Instead, he found himself staring into the barrel of Merrill's gun.

The seasoned agent met Jake's eyes and calmly said. "Sorry, Jake."

CHAPTER TWENTY

The chill in Jake's spine became a flood of shock that coursed through his entire body. He stared at Merrill, unable to form words, unable to even form a thought. Merrill too?

"Hands on top of your head, Jake."

Jake didn't move, still unable to process what he had just discovered. Merrill was a traitor?

Merrill sighed. "Please don't make me shoot you, Jake."

Finally, Jake's mind registered the truth. His blood began to boil, and his eyes narrowed. He shifted his weight slightly, preparing to lunge for the gun. Merrill's trained eyes caught the movement, though, and before Jake could react, he lowered his weapon and shot Jake just above the knee.

Jake cried out, and before he could recover from the shot, Merrill slammed into him and threw him to the ground onto his stomach. He started to roll over, but stopped when he felt the barrel of Merrill's weapon press against the base of his skull.

"I hate to do this, Jake," he said, "but I really don't have a choice."

"Yes, you do. There's always a choice."

Merrill planted his knee into Jake's back and held his supervisor still while he handcuffed him. "If you want to be pedantic, yes. So I guess the real answer is that I love my wife more than I love my country."

"What? What the hell are you talking about?"

"Stand up."

"Merrill, does Bard have your wife? Talk to me. I can help you."

Merrill sighed. "Stand up, or I'll shoot you in the back of the head. I'm not going to play games with you."

"You're not going to get away with this," Jake said. "What happens when the other agents find out?"

"The other agents are dead, or they will be shortly. You and Jess will be left alive at Bard's request."

"What? Are you serious?"

The door opened, and Dana Porter walked into the room. She glared down at Jake, a sneer on her face. Seeing her unbound, a gun in her hand, Jake knew the truth of what Merrill had said. He looked through the door and saw Franz wrapping Gutierrez's body in a sheet.

Dana drew her leg back and kicked Jake viciously in the jaw. His head snapped back, and stars swam across his vision. Her second kick landed in his ribs, and he doubled over, gasping as pain surged through his torso.

She brought her leg up to stomp on his head, but Merrill grabbed her and shoved her back against the wall. "Enough! Bard wants them alive and damaged only as much as necessary."

"That was necessary," Dana said. She smiled impishly. "He resisted me."

Merrill didn't return her smile. What he did instead was place his weapon under her chin. Her smile vanished immediately.

"I'm going to get the money I need to pay for my wife's treatment, Dana. You're going to help me, or you're going to die. I have no problem killing all three of you if you make trouble. Understand?"

Dana's upper lip trembled, and her eyes flashed fire, but she forced herself to stay calm. "I understand."

"Good. Go help the others with the bodies. Jake, stand up."

Jake struggled to his knees, his wounded leg screaming at him. Merrill realized this and hauled Jake to his feet. "Walk."

Jake limped forward. Franz grinned at him as he hefted Gutierrez's bound body onto a bunk. Coulson was dead too, a red hole in between his eyes where someone—probably Merrill—had shot him.

In the main cabin, Melina Vox sat at Jess's computer. Jess sat bound on the couch, her lip split and a bruise forming over her left eye.

"How are we looking, Vox?" Merrill asked.

Melina shook her head. "The firewalls on this thing are insane. I had an easier time breaking into the White House than I am breaking into this."

"Can you do it?"

"With three hours, I can."

"Three hours is just fine. We'll need some time to give Drew a chance to deal with our escorts. Has Captain Sontag been secured?"

"Trent has him under control. He's playing along."

Jake's shoulders slumped. "Trent too, huh?"

"Trent's daughter has stage four lymphoma," Merrill said. "My wife has stomach cancer. Thirty-six years old, and she's dying of stomach cancer because Secret Service insurance won't cover the treatment she needs. So now you know why." He turned back to Melina. "What about the chef?"

"He's been terminated. We left his body and Patel's in Trumbull's quarters."

"We can keep them there for now. That's fine."

"Merrill," Jake said, "I can help you. This can still be resolved. Don't do this. Don't betray your country."

Merrill spun to Jake, his eyes filled with venom. "Fuck my country! Seventeen years of service to my country, and the thanks I get is to let my wife die?"

"Let me help you."

"You can't help me. I filed grievances and appeals and letters to everyone. I talked to HR, to the insurance provider, the hospital; I even wrote a letter to the President." Jake's eyes widened. "That's right. I wrote a letter to your buddy Bryan asking him to please help my wife, and I got a form letter back. A fucking form letter, Jake. 'We regret to inform you… appreciate your service… fuck your wife, we don't give a shit.' So my country can go to hell, and as far as I'm concerned, you can follow it. Nothing personal, but this is my wife, Jake. This is my world."

"Let me talk to Bryan."

"You'll get your chance in a few minutes. You can all talk about whatever you want to talk about. But this is happening."

"What would your wife say if she knew?" Jake challenged. "Do you think this is what she would want?"

Merrill chuckled. "I think she would want not to die. For the record, she doesn't know. The last thing she needs right now is some asshole interrogating her or God forbid, imprisoning her because her husband cares enough to do whatever it takes to save her."

"Why didn't you tell me?" Jake asked. "You're my friend, Travis."

"I'm your subordinate, Jake. Don't try to use my first name for the first time in four years, and act like that makes us friends. I didn't tell you because there's nothing you can do to help me."

"There is. I'm dating the President's daughter. I can get her to talk to her dad. We can work something out."

"It's worked out. I'm going to give you, Jess, the President and his family to Bard."

"How are you going to do that when the plane's going to explode when it lands?"

"It's not going to explode when it lands. It's going to land, and I'm going to take all of you into custody."

"How do you plan to do that?" Jess asked. "Do you think you're just going to walk onto Hickam Air Force Base with the President of the United States in captivity and they're just going to let you get away?"

"It's not going to Hickam Air Force Base."

"You realize that the Air Force is monitoring us, right? Even if you 'deal with the escorts' the Air Force is still going to know where we are."

"We have a plan to handle that. What you need to know is that all of you will be expected to remain in this room. Franz? Dana?" The two terrorists walked into the main cabin. "Bring the Jacksons out here. Be careful. The President has military experience. It's possible he's slipped his bonds."

The two terrorists headed for the stateroom. Jake allowed himself a moment of absurd hope that maybe the President *had* slipped his bonds and could manage to get a weapon from Dana and turn the tide back in their favor.

But that hope died almost immediately. Jake couldn't allow himself to rely on fantasy. He needed a plan, a real plan, to get control of the situation again.

Try as he might to focus on recovering from this, he couldn't get past the betrayal. Trent and Merrill? The two most loyal agents Jake had ever worked with, and *they* were the traitors?

Maybe it was true that they weren't friends. Jake wasn't very good at making friends. After losing Drew to a court-martial and carrying around guilt for that event and for the events that prompted the court-martial, he hadn't sought companionship of any kind. He kept in touch with Max, but if he was honest, Max was more of a father figure than a friend. The President was sort of his friend before his Presidency, but their professional relationship had taken precedence for the past four and a half years. He considered Jess his friend, but they never saw each other outside of work.

He finally pushed those thoughts from his mind. It didn't matter right now. They were traitors to their country, not to Jake personally. Jake sympathized with their family situations, but that didn't excuse a choice to rob hundreds of other families of their loved ones, not to mention the consequences of turning the President of the United States over to a known domestic terrorist turned international terrorist who had flagrantly killed thousands of civilians already.

Jake heard screaming, and his eyes snapped ahead. He saw Dana leading the President into the stateroom. Ahead of him, Franz had one hand on Carrie's shoulder and his other arm wrapped around Sheila's neck. He was laughing and whispering something into Sheila's ear, and that was why Sheila had screamed.

Jake was on his feet before his mind registered what he was doing. He didn't feel the pain in his leg, so focused was he on reaching Sheila and rescuing her from the asshole who was hurting her.

So focused that he didn't notice Merrill moving until the traitorous agent's arms wrapped around his neck. Before he could respond, Merrill twisted and threw Jake over his hip. Jake crashed onto his back onto the deck and once more found himself staring into the barrel of Merrill's gun.

"Secure the Jacksons, then tie Mercer's ankles and wrists together behind his back," Merrill commanded.

"With pleasure," Dana said with a grin.

"You're a coward," Jake spat at Merrill.

"If you say so."

Merrill showed not a trace of guilt, not a trace of anger.

"Travis—" Jess began.

"Don't you *dare* use my first name!" Merrill snarled, not taking his eyes off of Jake. "You barely look at anyone besides Jake. Don't act like you give a shit about me. You're too busy swooning over him to give a crap about anyone else."

Out of the corner of his eye, Jake caught Sheila glancing over at Jess as Franz tied her and her parents together. Jess's lips thinned slightly, but she kept her cool. "Merrill," she began again. "Think about this. Do you really think Bard is going to help your wife? Do you really think he gives a damn what happens to her? Or to you?"

"No. But I think he's pragmatic. He knows that I can help him. So he'll come through with the money because he realizes that he needs to in order to get what he wants from me."

"And after you turn us over to him? What then?"

"He doesn't get any of you until my wife recovers."

Jake chuckled. "You're insane. What's your plan? Keep us hidden in the jungle somewhere until Bard tells you your wife's all better, then you turn us over?"

"More or less. I'm not just going to rely on Bard's word, so you can save the argument about him deceiving me."

"What about the argument that he will absolutely kill you if you try to blackmail him?"

"I'll die for my wife a thousand times over. I don't mind if she never knows why."

Jake realized there was no getting through to Merrill. His fear and resentment had poisoned any part of him that cared about doing the right thing.

"What if it were Sheila?" Merrill added. "What if it were the woman *you* love? Would you really let her die when you could do something to save her?"

Jake sighed. "I would do everything I could. But not this. I wouldn't do this."

Sheila looked from Jess over to Jake. Jake couldn't completely read her expression with her mouth taped shut, but her eyes communicated hurt.

He didn't have time to deal with that right now. He had to keep them safe, and the chances of doing that were fading fast.

If they hadn't disappeared already.

CHAPTER TWENTY ONE

"Raven One, this is Air Force One."

Jake could only glare at Merrill as the traitor spoke into Jess's commandeered headset. He was bound at his wrists and ankles, and both pairs of joints were bound together behind his back. Two strips of duct tape covered his mouth, and several layers of duct tape wrapped his head from underneath his chin to the crown of his head, keeping his jaw shut tightly so he couldn't even utter a muffled shout.

Jess was bound similarly to his left, and to his right, the Jackson's were tied back to back with a length of cord that the terrorists had cut from one of the parachutes stowed in the emergency locker behind the relief cabin. Sheila met Jake's eyes, and the terror in her expression was outweighed only by the fact that he couldn't do anything about it.

Jake couldn't hear what Raven One was saying, but Merrill's responses made the conversation clear.

"I'm sorry to say that Special Agent Mercer is deceased. The President's personal chef turned out to be a co-conspirator." A pause. "Special Agent Travis Merrill. My ID number is four-zero-nine-zero-seven. You can confirm that with the Secret Service." Another pause. "Of course."

A much longer pause. While Merrill waited, presumably for Raven One to verify his identity, Jake turned to the President's family. Sheila began to cry softly. Her mouth was duct-taped, and the sound was muffled almost to the point of silence, but tears streamed down her face, and Jake could see the anguish in her eyes.

Carrie glared at him with every ounce of the hate she had expressed when she told him when she said she wished she had died. For the first time, Jake actually believed he deserved it. He hadn't betrayed the President, and he had done everything he possibly could to keep them safe.

But it wasn't enough. They weren't safe. They had been betrayed, and the terrorists were winning. Innocent men were dead, and her family was bound in a neat little package to be delivered to terrorists. It didn't matter that Jake had done his best. There was no such thing as a participation prize in the Secret Service. You either succeeded or failed.

Jake had failed.

The First Lady's glare hurt. Sheila's tears hurt more. But what hurt worst of all was the look in Bryan's face.

He looked defeated. He had given up. The President of the United States, the leader of the free world, had resigned himself to becoming the property of a terrorist. He had resigned himself to his wife's and daughter's likely deaths. He had lost faith.

Jake knew that at the end of the day, the President was only human, but just like Jake had no option of failure in his job, the President had no option of quitting. He was the symbol of democracy, not just for America but for the world. To see him reduced to this state showed more clearly than anything just how much Jake had failed.

The free world rested in his hands, and he had let it slip through his grasp.

"I'm here," Merrill said. "Outstanding." His face paled, and Jake felt another flash of hope. "Of course. I'll see if I can bring him here for you."

He tapped the earpiece and slammed it onto the table. "Dammit!"

"Hey, easy!" Melina said. "I can't replace that if you break it."

"They want to talk to the President," Merrill said tightly. "They won't just take my verified ID and my word for it."

Jake's heart lifted. He might not survive this—hell, none of them likely would—but Merrill would have a hell of a time convincing anyone that the President was still safe with all of them bound and none of them willing to cooperate.

Then Merrill looked at Sheila, and the extent of his desperation became known.

Jake's spirits sank again, and he tried to cry out, but the bonds held firm. Merrill stood and drew his weapon. Carrie and Sheila both paled and shrieked, but their bonds muffled the noise.

Bryan didn't even lift his head.

Merrill pressed his handgun against Sheila's temple, and said in a low and deadly voice, "Both of you stop screaming, or I'll shoot Sheila."

Their cries softened to sobs, and Merrill cocked the hammer. "Quiet."

Sheila took a deep breath and managed to silence her sobs, so only her shaking shoulders indicated the fear she felt. Still holding the gun on Sheila, Merrill turned to the President. "I'm going to take your gag off. You're going to convince Raven One that all is well, or I'll kill your daughter and your wife. Do you understand me?"

Bryan nodded, just barely, but enough that Jake could see it.

Merrill could too. "Good. Melina, put the headset on the President's head."

Melina complied. As soon as the headset was secure, Merrill yanked the tape off of his mouth. Bryan winced and grunted, then took a deep breath. "Raven One, this is the President. No, young man, I'm fine."

Jake's heart fell through the floor and out of the airplane to dissipate in the wind. The President continued, doing an admirable job of seeming calm. "The Secret Service has the plane under control, and to my knowledge, that was the last of the terrorists. We should reach Hickam Air Force Base in"—he looked at Merrill, who held up three fingers—"three hours. Thank you for all of your help, son. I'll see to it that you're recognized for your service."

Merrill took the headset back and said, "So that's the plan. We're still heading to Hickam Air Force Base. Yes. I'll keep you posted. Okay. Over and out."

Jake stared at Bryan in disbelief. It was one of the most important rules of the nation that the United States didn't cooperate with terrorists. Yet here the President was doing exactly that.

Would you seriously rather he let Merrill shoot Sheila? He's not bluffing.

Jake wanted to be angry at Bryan, but he couldn't. The truth was he would have made the same decision if he was in the same circumstances. As much as he might like to believe that he would do the right thing regardless of the cost, the fact was that some costs were too high to accept.

He could understand now why Merrill had done what he had done. It sickened him to understand that, but he did.

"All right," Merrill said, handing the headset back to Melina, "that's done. Do you think you could impersonate Special Agent Foster?"

"I can do Special Agent Foster with a plugged nose after getting hit by one of us in the struggle. That'll have to work."

"That'll work. Any news on the escorts?"

Melina tensed a little. "It's no good. The satellites are all shut off."

"Can we *un*shut them off?"

She shook her head. "The CIA raided the control facility and left a dozen people there to guard it. NORAD switched the satellite system to standby, and the only way to switch it back is from NORAD satellite control."

"We have a guy there, don't we?"

"I don't know. He's gone quiet for the past six hours. It wouldn't matter anyway, because we have no way of commandeering the satellite if we can't get a signal to it."

Merrill sat and ran his hands through his head. Jake took slight encouragement knowing that Merrill's plan wasn't so foolproof as he had thought, but the other side of that coin was that Merrill might grow even more desperate and become unpredictable.

Jake wished he wasn't gagged. If he could talk to Merrill now, then he might be able to get through to him. He was certain that he could get Merrill's wife the treatment she needed if Merrill agreed to abandon the plan and get the President to safety. He could get treatment for Trent's daughter too. Both men together were more than capable of overcoming the terrorists, and Jake would see to it that they were treated fairly when they got home. Fairly, unfortunately, would mean the death penalty for treason, but they would be comfortable awaiting their execution date, and their loved ones would be cared for.

But he couldn't talk. Maybe that was by design. He had gagged the terrorists to prevent them from communicating with each other and formulating a plan. It made sense that Merrill had done the same.

Trent walked into the room, and Jake got a look at the third Secret Service traitor for the first time since learning of his betrayal. He looked disheveled. His hair was a sweaty mop, and his eyes were bloodshot. His hands trembled slightly as he handed Merrill a cup of coffee. Clearly he was having a harder time with what they were doing than Merrill was.

"What the hell?" Dana said. "I don't get coffee?"

"Go make some," Trent said without looking at her. "I'm not your butler."

Dana glared and stuck her middle finger at him, but she went to go make the coffee. That told Jake that the two Secret Service agents were in charge.

"Hey, bring me one too!" Franz called.

"You can make your own damned coffee," Dana called. "I'm not your bitch."

Franz grinned lecherously. "That's not what you said two nights ago."

“I was high two nights ago,” Dana said pertly. “I can’t be held accountable for what I said.”

“That’s fine,” Franz replied. He turned his grin to Sheila. “I can find a new girl.”

Sheila shuddered, and Franz laughed. He turned to Jake and said, "Hey, Mercer, what do you think? Is she a good girl? She nice and sweet?"

“Cut it out,” Merrill said. “For God’s sake, act like adults, you two.”

“Oh, my apologies, sir,” Franz replied mockingly. “Are we not mature enough to be terrorists?”

“Freedom fighters,” Melina corrected. “Use the right word.”

“Speak for yourself,” Franz retorted before smiling at Sheila again. “I like them afraid.”

Sheila whimpered, and when Franz caressed her cheek, she flinched back. Her bonds kept her from going too far, and when Franz’s fingertips finally reached her, she sobbed.

Jake would have given the rest of his life in a heartbeat for a chance to be free of his bonds right now.

He heard a muffled grunt and turned to see that Jess had fallen over and was now rolling toward the table. Merrill frowned and stopped her with his foot. He reached down and grabbed the cord tied between her ankle and wrist cuffs, then dragged her to the corner of the room and set her so she was balanced by the two walls. “If you roll over again, and the plane isn’t plummeting to the sea when you do, I’ll know you did it on purpose,” he said, “and I’ll shoot you.”

Jess kept her gaze lowered and nodded softly. As soon as Merrill turned back, though, she met Jake’s eyes and winked.

Jake wasn’t sure what the wink was for at first, but a moment later, he heard the faintest scraping noise. Jess winked again and Jake understood.

She was cutting her bonds.

CHAPTER TWENTY TWO

"Look, they're not going to shoot us down with the President on board," Melina argued. "We have time to think of something."

"They're not going to let us get away with the President on board either," Merrill countered, "and we don't have time. We're on three engines. We can't stay up indefinitely. If Sontag wasn't some kind of super pilot, we'd probably be in the water already."

"I thought Air Force One could stay airborne for up to a week," Dana said.

"With four engines, no missing doorway and no damage to the right wing, continual refueling and a full aircrew with relief pilots included, yes, it could. We have almost none of those things."

"I can fly the plane," Dana said. "So can Melina and Franz. Why is Sontag alive, anyway?"

"Because they know that you're all terrorists. They have to think that you three are in custody, and Sontag is still in charge of the aircraft."

"What's the worst that can happen?" Franz asked. "Like Melina said, they can't shoot us down. We can fly wherever we want. What are they going to do? Follow us to China?"

"Yes. Absolutely. And if China knows what's good for them, they will cooperate fully. This is the President of the United States. We will start World War Three in a heartbeat to get him back."

"I think you're overreacting," Melina said. "China might cooperate, but they're not just going to let USAF fighters shoot Air Force One down over their country. They'll send their own fighter jets to guide us to land, and—"

"And immediately capture us. Best case scenario, they send us to a Chinese prison and probe me and Trent for state secrets while they claim we died resisting arrest. The President goes home, and Air Force One gets dismantled for parts, but it's the old model anyway, so who cares?" Merrill steepled his fingers and looked ahead toward the cockpit. "We need those escorts to go away. I don't know how, but it needs to happen."

"Well, I don't know how you plan to make that happen," Melina said. "From what I've heard, there's nothing that can shoot an F-35 down except an F-22 and a satellite, and we have neither of those."

Jake heard a slight cough and risked a look at Jess's way. She looked down at her hands, and Jake followed her eyes to see her holding what looked like a bobby pin with one edge filed down into a thin blade.

Her bonds were cut. Her cuffs were still on, but the rope that tied her wrists and ankles behind her back had been severed.

Jake felt a leap of hope once more. If he could get his own bonds cut, they had a fighting chance. Not a great one with the cuffs still on and all five terrorists armed, but a chance.

He looked back at the terrorists. Dana, Melina and Merrill all faced each other. Franz was supposed to be guarding them, but he was turned toward the speakers as well.

Jake quickly and quietly shuffled over to Jess and reached as far as he could, which wasn't much more than opening his fingers and twisting his wrist her direction. He had to get so close that he was essentially leaning against her, but finally, he was able to get his hands around the makeshift knife.

Merrill looked their way just as Jake righted himself. Jess shut her eyes and shook, squeezing tears out as she pretended to sob. Jake looked toward her and did his best to appear to be comforting her. He hoped the terrorists wouldn't question why he was now four feet to the left of his previous position.

Merrill took the bait. "Damn. You two really liked each other. It's too bad you never saw where that could go. You two make a lot more sense than you and Sheila."

Sheila sobbed again at this, and Jake hated that he couldn't do anything to reassure her right now.

Soon. I just need to get us out of this, and then everything will be all right.

That wasn't true, though. He might save their lives and bring the terrorists to justice, but he knew that nothing would truly be all right until Bard was stopped. Even then, would he and Sheila survive a relationship that was marked by more trauma than anything else?

He shook the thoughts from his head. That was a concern for later.

He shifted position to sit upright and began sliding Jess's knife along the ropes binding his cuffs.

"What if we send a distress signal?" Dana said, "We change course wherever it is you want to go. You claim that the escorts ordered you to fly that way. They're the traitors, and they threatened to shoot the plane down if we don't comply. Then the Air Force sends interceptors to take the escorts out, and we're home free."

Merrill sighed and rubbed his temples. "I don't have time to explain all the reasons that won't work," he said. "But it won't."

"Okay, so let's just give up then," Dana snapped. "Here, I'll go make a sign that says, 'We surrender!' and hold it out the window so the fighter pilots can see. Should we do that instead?"

"I'm not in the mood, Dana," Merrill warned. "Don't push it."

"Well, I'm just trying to help. You're the Secret Service guy. You're supposed to know how all this works."

Merrill steepled his fingers and tapped them together again. "You're right about one thing. They won't shoot us down. If we land in the right place, we can get the prisoners somewhere before the entire U.S. military falls on us. If we can disappear in the right place, we can hide somewhere they won't find us and then find a way to get to Bard. It's a risk, but it might be the only chance we have."

"Where is the right place, though?"

"Somewhere like the South Asian jungle. Myanmar or Vietnam. We can hide in the forest, and effectively disappear. Those nations don't have the infrastructure China does, so they can't find us easily, and the United States will have an even harder time getting inside."

"I thought you said they wouldn't mind starting World War Three," Franz challenged.

"That was a bit of an exaggeration. If the nations involved cooperate with them—and they definitely will—then the U.S. will work with them to find the President. There will be U.S. boots on the ground, but it will be a collaborative effort, not an actual war."

Melina pursed her lips. "You don't think they'd try to force a water landing? We'll run out of fuel before we reach Vietnam. They might just wait for us to run out of fuel and then pick the President up out of the water before we ditch the plane."

"They won't force us to ditch. We won't play along with that. We'll hold the plane at twenty thousand feet, and if we run out of fuel, we'll just drop like a rock. As long as we're in control of the aircraft, the President's fate is in our hands. That's a good point about fuel, though. We'll need a reason to refuel again."

He drummed his fingers on the table a moment, then tapped his earpiece. "Trent? It's Merrill. Listen, we're going to make a break for Myanmar and crash land in the jungle somewhere, then head off the grid until we can find a way to get the prisoners to Bard." There was a brief pause, then he said tersely. "If you have a better idea, I'd love to hear it. Yeah, me either. So here's what I need. Tell the captain to make up a reason why we need more fuel. I don't know, some sort of malfunction or something. Here, I've got it. Tell him to start dumping fuel and make a panicked call saying that the fuel system is compromised, probably as a result of the earlier EMP attack that fried aircraft systems. Have him stop dumping fuel with enough left over to give us time to refuel, then tell them that we need fuel. Tell them we want full tanks just in case that crap happens again. Once we're refueled, we're just going to make a break for it. We won't tell them where we're going, we'll just go. They won't shoot us down with the President on board."

Another pause. "Yes. We're going to set the plane down somewhere in the jungle, then move our asses as fast as possible deeper inside. It will take the U.S. a long time to put together a real search and rescue."

Another pause. "Come on, Trent, we've taken survival training. We have a ton of gear, and we have three people who can help carry it. We'll leave Sheila bound and keep a gun to her head at all times so the prisoners are motivated to walk. If any of them act stupid, we shoot them. If we have to, we shoot Sheila and make Carrie our next guinea pig. No, it's not ideal, but Bard will forgive us for losing Sheila if he gets the President and Jake."

And me? Jake thought. *Why the hell am I so important?*

Maybe one day, he'd get a chance to ask Bard that question in person.

"Speaking of Jake, he used to be a Marine, and he worked as a sniper with SEAL teams. He has real survival experience. He'll help us out as long as he knows Sheila will die if he doesn't."

A final pause, then, "Nut the fuck up, Trent. You're all in now. There's no bargaining for an easier sentence. Think of your daughter, and let's get this shit done. We knew this ended with both of us dead before we helped Bard escape."

Jake's eyes widened. How had he not thought of that before?

While Jake and Jess were pursuing Hadad, Bard had tried to recruit Jake over to his side. Instead, Jake had taken Bard into custody. Despite Jake's best efforts to ensure that the terrorist remained captured, he had escaped on his way to a CIA detention facility. The official report was that the convoy had been ambushed by Trident operatives. Apparently, there had been Secret Service traitors among those operatives.

A moment later, Merrill sighed. "Awesome. Melina? Give me the headset."

Melina handed him the communicator, and Merrill called, "Raven One, this is Air Force One. We seem to be experiencing a problem—oh, you're talking to the Captain? All right. I'll let you handle it."

He set the headset down and shrugged. "Worked like a charm. They'll have the tanker in position in ten minutes."

"Do you think the plane will make it all the way to Vietnam without breaking apart?" Melina asked.

"It has to."

Jake continued to work steadily at the rope. The sharpened bobby pin was the most awkward cutting tool he had ever used and about as effective as a disposable butter knife. Several times, Jake had nearly dropped it, each time causing his heart to pound. If they lost that bobby pin, then it was all over.

But it was cutting through the cord slowly but surely. Finally, Jake heard a soft twang as the rope gave way. He tensed, preparing for the terrorists to react to the noise, but they didn't.

He looked at Jess and saw in her eyes the same determination he felt.

Okay, Jake. Time to see what you're really made of.

CHAPTER TWENTY THREE

Jake looked around and noted the positions of the terrorists. Franz remained where he was, leaning against the wall and alternating between leering at Sheila, leering at Dana and looking bored. He would be Jake's first target. He was nearest to Jake, and while he wasn't much of a fighter, he was more of a threat than either of the women were. Dana would be next on his list. She stood next to the wall on the other side of the hallway, picking her fingernails and doing her best to look like a badass thug. Jess could take her, even with her hands and ankles cuffed.

The problem was Merrill and Melina. Melina didn't give Jake a very strong impression of her fighting skills either, but she was smart. She would be the one who would think to back away and fire at them from a distance.

And Merrill was a trained Secret Service Agent who had bested Jake physically already. Granted, he had a gun the first time, and Jake was cuffed the second time, but Jake was cuffed now, and even if he wasn't, Merrill was armed, and it would take all of Jake's attention to handle him, let alone him and three other combatants.

He needed Merrill to leave. If Merrill was otherwise occupied, he could handle Dana and Franz, and Jess could handle Melina.

Merrill tapped his earpiece. "Are we refueled, Trent? Wonderful. Wait until the tanker is clear, then tell Sontag to take us to Vietnam. What do you mean, what if he refuses? We have three other pilots here. They're already going to know something is wrong once we're on our way to Vietnam. In fact, just kill Sontag once the tanker is clear. I'll send Dana up front to fly."

He nodded at Dana, and Dana headed toward the cockpit. "Finally. I owe Sontag for staring at my breasts the entire time we were in the cockpit together."

"Can you really blame him?" Franz called.

Dana didn't respond.

"Okay, Dana's on her way, Trent. As soon as she's in the cockpit, shoot Sontag. I'll stay on the line until you tell me Dana's at the controls."

Jake felt a pang of grief. He needed Trent and Dana to be unaware of the struggle until he took out Franz, Melina and Merrill. He couldn't do anything to save Sontag.

A moment later, he heard a muffled crack. Sheila flinched and burst into tears. Bryan hung his head.

"Is it done?" Merrill asked. "Wonderful. All right, you hang out there with her. I'm going to make some coffee and breakfast for all of us. We have a long flight ahead of us."

Jake felt a rush of excitement. That would leave just Franz and Melina for them to deal with. That was easily doable.

Merrill stood and handed Melina the headset as the plane started to bank. Merrill had a lot of experience on the jet and easily maintained his balance, but Franz fell over and cursed when he hit his head against the wall. "Dammit! A little warning next time?"

"Sit down if you can't keep your feet," Merrill said. "Melina, I expect our escorts to start pitching a fit any second now. Do me a favor and tell them that we're in control of the plane now, and we're going to go where we want to go. Don't give them any more details than that. Just tell them we're not going to comply anymore."

"Will do."

She took the headset, and Merrill started for the galley.

Close the door, Jake prayed. *Please close the door.*

Merrill opened the door to the galley and walked inside.

Then closed the door behind him.

Jake sprang instantly into action, getting to his feet and slamming his shoulder into Franz. The surprised terrorist tried to call for help, but Jake's strike knocked the air from his lungs. Behind him, he heard Melina start to cry out before her cry was muffled.

Jake couldn't look back to see how Jess was faring. He could only focus on Franz. The terrorist planted a hand on Jake and pushed him off. Jake allowed Franz to help him to his feet, then dropped his knee down onto Franz's throat, slamming the terrorist to the ground and holding him there. He could hear a few bumps behind him and prayed that Merrill wouldn't hear the noise and come out to investigate.

Franz struggled underneath Jake, and Jake put all of his weight onto Franz's neck. The terrorist's face turned red, then purple as he fought to no avail. He pushed and shoved and scratched, but Jake used his years of training and experience to hold the position and put even more pressure onto Franz's neck.

Franz began to choke and gurgle as his body struggled ineffectually for oxygen. God, it took so long, though. At any moment, Merrill or Trent or Dana could come out, and it would be all over. Or Melina would get the better of Jess, and Jake would earn a bullet to his brain for his trouble.

Finally, after what seemed like an eternity, Franz stilled. His eyes glazed over, and after a few weak slaps to Jake's face, his arm fell limp at his side.

Jake remained where he was and counted to sixty, not wanting to leave any chance that the terrorist would survive. He was just about to stand when he heard Jess whisper. "I'm right behind you. Don't freak out."

The next instant, he felt a key slide into his handcuffs and pop them open the ankle cuffs followed, and Jake grabbed Franz's gun and stood. He turned to Jess, who reached up for the duct tape and whispered, "This will hurt."

She tore the tape off, and he breathed in sharply as a stinging sensation radiated over his face. He could feel wetness on his cheeks and knew that he was bleeding.

But that was a small price to pay for the chance they now had. He turned to the President and his family and said softly. "I'll untie you after we take this airplane back. Hold tight. Jess? Get on the headset, but don't say anything to the escorts until I give the all-clear. I don't want the others to overhear."

"What about Merrill, Trent and Dana?"

"I'll take care of them."

"All three of them? No, if I can't talk to the escorts until they're killed anyway, then I'm going to help you."

Jake couldn't think of a good argument to that. "All right. Follow my lead, then."

He headed toward the galley and motioned for Jess to cross to the other side of the door. He wanted nothing more than to take over now, but it was safer and smarter to wait for Merrill to leave the room—probably with his hands full of food—then take him out.

Actually, better idea. He needed Merrill to get into the cockpit. He'd capture him and threaten him at gunpoint to get him into the cockpit. Once he was inside, he would do what he needed to do.

The door opened, and Merrill stepped outside carrying two drink trays, one with three coffees, the other with two. Jake pressed his gun to Merrill's temple, and when the traitor stiffened, Jess stepped in front of him and hissed, "Don't even think about it."

Merrill chuckled bitterly. "Dammit. Goddammit. How the hell did you get out?"

"I'll tell you later," Jake replied. "Right now, you need to get me into the cockpit."

"You fucking asshole," Merrill continued, ignoring Jake. "What are you, a freaking superhero? Just my damned luck that Dawson goes on vacation this week. With that runt in charge, I take this plane hour one, no problems."

"Moan, moan," Jake said. "Cockpit now, or you never see your wife again."

Merrill He met Jake's eyes, and the purity of the hate in his gaze almost unnerved Jake. "Of course, I'm never going to see her again. You just killed her. You just killed the best woman who's ever lived. You asshole."

"I'll get her the help she needs," Jake promised. "You have my word. Whether you help me or not, I'll make sure she survives." Jess shot him a glance, but Jake kept his eyes on Merrill. "All you have to decide is whether or not you get to see that or whether you die right here and never know."

Merrill's gaze faltered. Then he lowered his eyes. He nodded, and Jake breathed a sigh of relief.

Then Merrill threw the coffee at Jake and went for his gun.

Jess fired twice. Jake heard the shots but didn't see them. The coffee seared his face, and though he had closed his eyes before the hot liquid could burn them, his eyelids felt like they were on fire.

He stumbled backward, and when he did open his eyes, he saw Merrill on the ground, one hand clutched to his neck. Candy-red blood spurted through his fingers, and he stared at Jake with the knowledge of death in his gaze.

"Take care of her," he wheezed. "Jeanie Merrill. Keep your promise."

Despite everything that had happened, Jake felt sympathy for Merrill. His actions were misguided in the extreme, but all he wanted to do was save the woman he loved.

Jake could understand that.

"I will," he told his former friend. "I promise."

Merrill gave Jake the ghost of a smile. Then he sighed and let his head fall. He didn't breathe again.

Jake sighed and reached down to close Merrill's eyes. Then he stood and looked at Jess. He could mourn Merrill properly later. They still had a plane to catch.

"We need to get into the cockpit," he said. "You can't talk to Raven One right now or Trent and Dana might here you, but you can send a text message to them."

"I can't text a fighter cockpit."

"Yes, you can. The F-35s can display text on their screens. Send it over the voice channel. All it will sound like is interference. They need to give the cockpit a reason to open the door. Tell them… I don't know, tell them to make up a legitimate sounding airplane emergency that would require one of them to go to the control room at the rear of the plane. I'll stand by the door and take out whoever exits, then rush the cockpit."

"How are you going to convince Dana to fly the plane?"

"She doesn't want to die. I could see that when I was interrogating her earlier. When she knows all of her allies are dead, she'll comply."

"What if she doesn't?"

"Then let's hope this isn't too much worse than flying a helicopter."

Jess didn't look happy with that, but it wasn't as though they had a choice. She nodded and headed to the computer.

Jake took up position in the relief cabin, gun aimed at the door.

The wait dragged on. Jake's training told him it had only been a few minutes, but it felt like an eternity. All of the ways this could fail ran through his mind: Jess wouldn't be able to get through to Raven One. Raven One wouldn't think to check for texts. Trent and Dana would pick up on the ruse and refuse to open the cockpit. Trent would get a lucky shot and get Jake before Jake could get him.

Grow the fuck up, Marine, Max's voice echoed in his mind. *Focus on the mission.*

He took a deep breath and steadied himself. He could do this. He had come this far.

The door opened, and Trent rushed out, his face white as a sheet. He barely had time to register Jake's presence before Jake put a bullet in his brain.

"What the hell?" Dana cried.

Jake rushed into the cockpit, and her eyes widened. She reached for her gun, and Jake rushed her. He caught her hand before she could pull her weapon and pressed the gun to her temple. "Do as I say, and you can survive this. Fight me, and I won't hesitate. Do you understand?"

Dana looked up at him, trembling with fear. "Do the right thing, Dana," Jake said.

Dana took a deep breath. Then her eyes hardened. "Go to hell."

She shoved the yoke forward, and Air Force One pitched down. Jake stumbled off balance, and Dana reached for her gun again. He twisted and fired. The bullet caught Dana in the temple, but the movement caused Jake to slide into the throttle. The engines roared to full power, and Jake heard Air Force One groan as the plane accelerated straight down.

Dawn broke over the Pacific just in time for Jake to see them hurtling toward the water at nine-tenths of the speed of sound.

CHAPTER TWENTY FOUR

He grabbed the yoke and pulled backward, but the yoke wouldn't respond. He tried the throttles, and the roaring calmed, but the groaning remained strong. He didn't know much about planes, but he knew that if their speed increased too much, they would break apart.

He grabbed the yoke again and yanked backward. The plane creaked in protest, and Jake prayed he wouldn't break them up leveling out.

Slowly, but surely, the plane leveled out. When Jake saw the horizon at the upper corner of his vision, he cheered, and when the nose was finally level, he sighed with relief. He looked around for a trim tab. He didn't even know if jets had trip tabs like helicopters, but he checked anyway.

They did have trim tabs, and when he found it, he set it to level.

The nose pitched slowly upward, and Jake pulled it to three degrees down. The nose leveled out again, and Jake sighed. "Okay. That's fine. We can do this."

He tapped his ear, then remembered he didn't have an earpiece. He fished for Dana's and pulled it out of the dead woman's ear and put it in his own ear, then tapped it.

"Jess, it's Jake. I have the plane."

"Good. Can I cut the President and his family loose now? They took a hard tumble when we did our little rollercoaster dive."

"Yes, cut them loose. Before you do that, transfer Raven One to the cockpit."

"Will do."

A moment later, Raven One said, "Air Force One?"

"This is Air Force One. We've regained control of the aircraft."

"Yeah, so you say. I don't know what the hell is going on in there, but the bottom line is you need to level out, turn around and head back to Hickam Air Force Base or God's wrath is gonna seem like a kiss from Grandma compared to what's going to happen to you."

"That is fine with me, Raven One. I have every intention of putting this plane down at Hickam Air Force Base and it'll be clear once that happens that I'm on your side. The problem is, I've flown a UH-1 once for twenty minutes, and that's about it. And I thought I was flying level."

"You're descending at three hundred feet a minute. Ten minutes of that, and you're going to fly into the Pacific."

"But my nose is pointing at the horizon."

"It should be three degrees above the horizon. Passenger jets don't fly at even pitch, they fly at a slight nose-up angle."

"Ah. That explains it." Jake set the trim tab to level again. "I guess level on the trim tab means level flight, not level nose."

"Yep." Raven One's voice sounded a lot calmer now that Air Force One was complying with his instructions. "Okay, I'm going to get you through this… is this Mercer?"

"Yeah, it's me."

"Damn. I want to hear that story later. Anyway, I'm going to get you through this, Mercer, but you need to do *exactly* as I tell you immediately and without question. I don't care what you think is right or wrong or what you think you see in or out of the aircraft, you need to do what I tell you to do the moment I tell you to do, or you *will* crash that airplane, do you understand?"

"Yes, sir."

"Outstanding. Step one. Pull the throttle lever marked four to the idle position. You're shooting fuel out of the hole where your outboard right engine used to be."

Jake looked for the throttle and pulled it to idle. The plane began to drift to the right, and Jake felt the pedals under his feet move as the trim tab directed the plane to compensate.

"Good. Now, just in front of the throttles on the instrument panel should be a series of toggle switches. Turn the one marked four off."

Jake did so, and Raven One said, "Good. You're not leaking fuel anymore. The next thing I need you to do is press the trim tab down and turn it into the off position."

Jake blinked. They had just leveled the plane, and Raven One wanted him to turn the trim tab off.

Do exactly *as I tell you immediately and without question.*

Jake took a deep breath and pressed the trim tab down. It depressed easily, and he moved it to the off position, then released it. It popped into place, and the plane began to drift to the right again.

"We're drifting, Raven One."

"I know. Stay calm. Airplanes want to fly straight and level, even when they've taken a beating. You won't spin out of control. Now look at your throttles and tell me what they're set to."

"Uh… looks like fifty percent for all of them."

"Okay. Move three to sixty percent for me."

Jake obliged. The airplane still drifted, but less noticeably than before.

"Now move one and two to forty-five percent."

He moved one and two halfway between forty and fifty. The drift slowed and then stopped.

"Great. You're doing great. Okay, pull the yoke back *slowly*, and stop when I tell you."

Jake slowly pulled the yoke back. The nose of the plane pitched up, and Jake felt an odd, weightless sensation as the tail dropped.

"Stop." He did, and Raven One said, "Now push the yoke back to neutral position. Keep going. Stop. You're going to hold that climb until you hit ten thousand feet."

"Are we slowing down? It feels like we're slowing down."

"You are, but that's okay. You were at five hundred knots before. By the time you reach ten thousand feet, you'll be at three hundred knots, and that's where I want you to stay."

"Okay."

"All right. While we're climbing, I'm going to tell you something that sounds scary. You need to stay calm for me."

"I am at your mercy, Raven One."

"Okay. When you were diving, you lost the top half of your fin."

"What fin?"

"The vertical part of your tail."

"Oh, lovely."

"Don't worry. The plane is still flyable, but it's going to lose a considerable amount of altitude and gain a considerable amount of speed when you turn because you'll have to use your elevators with less help from your rudder. That's why I'm having you climb."

"Got it."

"Second thing. I'm not taking you to Hickam. You're about three hours out from Hickam, and I don't know how much longer the airframe will hold out. I'm taking you to Henderson Field on Midway Atoll instead. That's about ten minutes away."

"That's good news."

"It is, and it isn't. It's hard to see Midway, and with only three engines and half a fin, you're not going to be able to go around. You'll get one chance to land, or you'll end up in the water. If that happens, don't panic. The Navy has rescue boats ready to come to you. But let's try not to make it happen, okay?"

"I'm fully in agreement."

"Okay. You're doing great, Jake. We've got this."

"Have I ever told you that I like you, Raven One?"

"It hasn't come up in conversation, but I figured you probably did. All right. Go ahead and push the yoke forward. Same thing, slow and stop when I tell you to."

Jake did, and the horizon slowly lifted.

"Stop."

Jake stopped, and the nose continued to pitch down. When the horizon was about ten degrees below the nose, Raven One said, "Pull back slowly."

Jake did, the nose pitched below the horizon, and Jake felt a rush of fear, but after a moment, the nose slowed, then began to lift.

"Push the yoke forward. Stop."

The nose tipped up to about three degrees above the horizon, then stopped.

"Excellent. Tell your passengers to strap down. We're going to turn steeply. Remember, you'll be losing altitude and gaining speed. Don't freak out. You're okay."

"Got it. Jess? Can you make sure the President and his family are belted in?"

"Got it."

Jess's voice was tense, and Jake couldn't blame her. His knuckles were white on the yoke. He took a breath and forced himself to relax.

"Okay, we're all set," Jess said. "Go for it, flyboy."

Jake laughed nervously. "All right, Raven One. Tell me what to do."

"Twist the yoke to the left like you're turning a steering wheel. The nose will start to pitch down. That's okay."

Jake turned, and the horizon tilted like a seesaw. As warned, the nose began to pitch down, and Jake heard more groaning as the plane's speed increased. When the horizon was tilted about forty degrees, Raven One said, "Now turn the yoke to neutral, relative to you, not the horizon."

Jake did that and watched anxiously as the horizon retreated to the upper right corner of the cockpit.

"You're doing great. Now pull the yoke back."

The groaning increased in noise, but Jake felt the nose respond as the massive plane banked.

"Stop. Now turn the yoke to the right, just like a steering wheel."

Jake did, and the wings leveled, but the horizon didn't appear. The groaning began to turn to a whine, and Jake's heart started to pound.

"Stay with me, Jake, you're doing great. Pull back on the yoke slowly."

Jake pulled back, and when he saw the horizon again, he released a breath he didn't realize he had been holding.

"Wonderful. Great job. You're doing wonderfully. Now stop. Good. Push the yoke forward now. And… stop. Go back to neutral. Excellent. Okay, you're at four hundred eighty knots and four thousand feet. We need to get your speed down to about two hundred knots before we can extend the landing gear, okay? Pull the throttles back to idle."

"Idle?"

"Yes. Trust me."

Jake pulled all three throttles steadily back to idle. The plane shimmied a little, but when all three throttles were at idle, it settled into a slight left drift.

"Okay. Set the left trim tab to… we'll say six degrees right."

"Where's the left trim tab?"

"Right next to the one you were using earlier. It may or may not be marked."

"It's marked. I see it. Setting to six degrees."

The drift stopped, and Raven One said, "Okay. That will keep you straight. You'll hit two hundred knots in about two minutes. When you hear a chime and see a green light above a switch labeled LANDING GEAR, hit that switch."

"Raven One," Jess said, "remember we don't have electronics."

"Right. Crap. Okay, that's fine. Just below that switch should be a small box. It looks like a smaller version of a thermostat."

"Yeah, I found it."

"Flip it open. There's a wheel inside. When I tell you to, start turning it clockwise until it clicks into place."

"Okay."

"All right. Once your gear are down, you'll be one minute away from touchdown. As soon as your gear is down, a lot of things need to happen at once. You need to pull the nose up to seven degrees. Then, you need to put your flaps all the way down. Do you see a bank of four slide toggles to your left? They look like toggles on a sound mixer."

"I see them."

"Okay. Those are your flaps. When I say so, push them all the way forward."

"Is this a bad time to say I hate that everything is backwards when you fly?"

"This is a perfect time to say that. You won't get another chance. When your flaps are down, you'll slow rapidly. You will continue to descend in a controlled manner, so don't panic. Ready? Five… four… three… two… one. Landing gear now."

Jake spun the wheel. It moved much faster than he expected, and he slowed down.

"Don't slow down. Go, go, go."

He sped up and heard a loud groan that did nothing to help his peace of mind. At the same time, he felt the plane slow as drag increased.

"Wonderful. Hit your flaps and pull the yoke back *very slowly*."

Jake did that, and Raven One said. "Flaps faster, yoke same speed. Good. Okay, push the yoke to neutral. Wonderful. Your nose is up a degree too much, but that's okay, you'll still make the runway."

"What runway?"

"It's there. Trust me. Now, a lot more has to happen when you touch down. *In this exact order*, you will turn off the left trim tab the same way you turned off the right. Then, you will push the throttles forward to twenty percent for three seconds before pulling them back to idle. During those three seconds, you will push the yoke very slightly forward. When you pull the throttles back, you will pull the yoke back to neutral. Once you feel your nose wheel touch down, three things need to happen at the same time. You will press the buttons on the front of throttles one, two and three. Those are your thrust reversers. You will slide the two slide toggles to the right of the flap toggles all the way forward. Those are your lift spoilers. You will flip the switch underneath those toggles that says WHEEL BRAKES. Those are self-explanatory."

"All right. Got—"

"Now. Trim tab."

Jake switched the trim tab off, wondering why he didn't feel the wheels touch down."

"Throttles." He pushed the throttles forward. Then the plane bucked left and right, and Raven One said, "Yoke forward now!"

Jake pushed the yoke forward a touch. "I'm doing it."

"Okay. Damn it. Pull the throttles back to idle."

Jake did it, but the plane still shook. "No good."

"Try pushing them forward again. We'll go around."

Jake did that, and Raven One asked, "Nothing?"

"You tell me. I pushed the throttles forward, what's happening?"

"Shit. They're stuck. The engines won't let you stop, but they won't let you slow down either."

"So what do we do?"

Raven One sighed. "We crash it."

"What?"

"It's not going to be hard enough to kill you, but if we don't get the plane stopped, you're going into the ocean, and that *will* kill you. Not to mention the President. Twist the yoke. We're going to run the right wing into the ground and spin the plane around."

"I feel like this is something we're supposed to avoid," Jake replied.

"No time to argue. Do it now."

Jake sighed and twisted the yoke. The wing came down, slowly at first, then hard.

It hit thc ground with a jarring crunch that Jake felt in his gums. The plane bounced sickeningly, then bounced again.

Jake's head flew forward, nearly impacting the yoke. The plane spun to the left, and once the direction of travel no longer forced air over the ailerons, friction slammed the left wing down onto the tarmac. This bump was much worse than the first one, and Jake clenched his teeth, waiting to feel them tip over into the ocean.

He held his breath as the massive plane slowed and finally stopped. Only then did he allow himself to look out of the cockpit window. He was on the runway, thirty yards from a strip of beach and the ocean beyond.

A moment later, Jake heard a roar and saw two F-35s zoom out over the ocean, their exhausts sending jets of water into the air. After a moment, they turned vertical and disappeared from Jake's view.

"Congratulations, Special Agent Mcrccr. You just earned your wings."

Jake laughed and slumped back in his chair, giddy with relief. A moment later, the chair spun around, and Jake saw Sheila's smiling face.

She kissed him deeply, and Jake didn't care that her parents were watching. He pulled her close and kissed her back just as passionately.

EPILOGUE

After the events of the past two days, Jake almost expected another catastrophe on the return trip. Instead, the twelve-hour trek from Midway to Washington D.C. turned out to be uneventful. The C-17 Globemaster was far less luxurious than Air Force One, but all four engines remained intact and none of the crew turned out to be terrorists, so that was a plus.

Raven One—Captain Thomas Anderson on the ground—shared a drink with Jake before they boarded the return flight and promised to visit Jake in Washington on his next leave, observing that Jake was a "damned good pilot for a jarhead."

Jake, in turn, promised to visit Thomas in Hawaii once he had Bard in custody, though he declined an offer to fly something "a bit faster."

"I'll leave that to the professionals. I'm a lot better at blowing things up."

"Spoken like a true Marine," Thomas replied.

The President and his family were treated for injuries at the hospital in Midway. Jake and Jess—as the only two surviving Secret Service Agents—remained at the First Family's side the entire time. Jake and Sheila didn't get to steal a moment alone, but Jake made no attempt to hide his affection behind a professional demeanor, and Bryan didn't seem to disapprove. Even Carrie tolerated the affection between the two, though it would be a stretch to say she had grown to like Jake.

Now they were descending toward Langley-Eustis Air Force Base, where Art was waiting with a brand-new group of hand-picked and thoroughly vetted agents to escort the President and his family home. Jake and Jess would be allowed to join the escort, then, Jake was almost certain, would be expected immediately back at headquarters for a thorough debriefing.

No rest for the righteous today.

As for the wicked?

"What's going to happen to Merrill's wife?" Jess asked.

"She's going to get the treatment she needs. Same with Trent's daughter. Bryan's going to pay for the treatments personally with his own money."

"What about their bodies? I mean, Merrill and Trent were assholes, but… I mean, I can understand why they did it. When you love someone, you'll do anything to protect them."

Jake thought of Sheila in the arms of the insane Vincent St. Clair. He had managed to save both the President and Sheila that time, but if he had to choose, would he really put his job ahead of his emotions? What if Sheila was dying of cancer and someone had a way to save her? Was there really a limit to what he would do? He would like to think so, but he couldn't honestly say for sure that there was.

That was why he had acted the way he did. "I asked Bryan to make sure that their bodies were returned to their families and that their involvement was kept quiet. As far as anyone will know, they died trying to protect the President from the terrorists."

Jess smiled at that. "That's good. I'm glad."

Jake offered the ghost of a smile, but that was all he could do.

They had beaten Trident this time, but Bard, Drew and Dalton were still out there. Once more, the instigators of everything that had happened in the past year would escape scot free leaving a trail of bodies in their wake. A smaller trail this time, but for the families of Bard's victims and collaborators, the number of the dead wouldn't matter. All that would matter is that their worlds had been suddenly and violently mangled because of the aspirations of one sadistic man.

"Better wipe that frown off your face before Sheila wakes up," Jess said. "She's going to need happy Jake for a while."

Jake lifted his eyes to his partner, who sat across from him, then lowered his eyes to Sheila, who rested peacefully, her head on Jake's lap. Her parents rested in a similar position, stretched out over multiple jump seats in the spartan freighter's hold.

"Yeah. I'll work on that. I'm just pissed off. Once more, Bard gets away."

"Yeah, I know. It pisses me off too."

Jake shook his head. "It feels worse this time, somehow. Even though fewer people died, it just feels more painful."

"Because of Trent and Mercer?"

Jake nodded.

"I know what you mean," Jess said. "I don't get it at all. I don't understand how you dedicate years of your lives to serving your country and protecting your President, and then all of a sudden, you just throw that all away. It makes no sense."

Jake brushed a lock of hair from Sheila's brow. She stirred, then settled once more onto his lap. "I get it," he said softly."

Jess lowered her gaze briefly. "Hey, about that."

"About what?"

"You, Sheila and me. What Merrill said. It's—"

"Oh, don't worry about that," Jake interrupted. "I didn't believe him for a moment. He wasn't thinking clearly. He hadn't been thinking clearly for a while. I know you don't have romantic feelings for me." He chuckled. "Could you imagine that? You and me together?" He laughed. "That would be crazy."

Jess smiled, but Jake thought he saw a hint of sadness in her eyes. "Yeah. Crazy."

The intercom buzzed, and Sheila stiffened and opened her eyes.

"Be advised, touchdown in Langley Eustis will occur in sixty seconds. Please sit in an upright position and hold onto the grab handles on either side of your chair."

The First Family sat up groggily. Carrie frowned as she gripped the grab handles. "This is seriously the best we can do for safety for our troops? Honey, you have to do something about this."

"I'll write a proposal to Congress," Bryan replied.

"Baby?" Sheila said groggily. "Where are we?"

Jake smiled and gently kissed the tip of Sheila's nose. "We're home, my love."

NOW AVAILABLE!

ABSOLUTE TREASON
(A Jake Mercer Political Thriller—Book #5)

"Thriller writing at its best."
--Midwest Book Review (*Any Means Necessary*)

From the #1 bestselling and USA Today bestselling author Jack Mars (with over 10,000 five-star reviews) comes a groundbreaking new political thriller series: when the President of the United States or his family are threatened, it is up to Jake Mercer, former Marine sniper turned Secret Service agent, to protect them from dangers—both foreign and domestic.

When the President visits Russia for a summit, his life is in danger, and Secret Service Agent Jake Mercer finds himself pitted against a rogue ex-KGB officer. Can he outsmart his cunning adversary before the ultimate checkmate?

"Thriller enthusiasts who relish the precise execution of an international thriller, but who seek the psychological depth and believability of a protagonist who simultaneously fields professional and personal life challenges, will find this a gripping story that's hard to put down."
--Midwest Book Review, Diane Donovan (regarding Any Means Necessary)

"One of the best thrillers I have read this year. The plot is intelligent and will keep you hooked from the beginning. The author did a superb job creating a set of characters who are fully developed and very much enjoyable. I can hardly wait for the sequel."
--Books and Movie Reviews, Roberto Mattos (re Any Means Necessary)

ABSOLUTE TREASON is the fifth book in a new series by #1 bestselling and critically acclaimed author Jack Mars, whose books have received over 10,000 five-star reviews and ratings. The series begins with ABSOLUTE THREAT (book #1).

A gripping and unpredictable political thriller, the Jake Mercer series is a page-turning action series that will leave you unable to put it down. This fresh and exciting action hero will have you turning pages late into the night, and fans of Brad Taylor, Vince Flynn, and Tom Clancy are sure to fall in love.

Future books in the series are also available!

Jack Mars

Jack Mars is the USA Today bestselling author of the LUKE STONE thriller series, which includes seven books. He is also the author of the new FORGING OF LUKE STONE prequel series, comprising six books; of the AGENT ZERO spy thriller series, comprising twelve books; of the TROY STARK thriller series, comprising seven books; of the SPY GAME thriller series, comprising ten books; of the JAKE MERCER thriller series, comprising seven books (and counting); and of the new TYLER WOLF thriller series, comprising seven books (and counting).

Jack loves to hear from you, so please feel free to visit www.Jackmarsauthor.com to join the email list, receive a free book, receive free giveaways, connect on Facebook and Twitter, and stay in touch!

BOOKS BY JACK MARS

TYLER WOLF THRILLER SERIES
DOUBLE AGENT (Book #1)
DOUBLE CROSS (Book #2)
DOUBLE ASSET (Book #3)
DOUBLE DOCTRINE (Book #4)
DOUBLE JEOPARDY (Book #5)
DOUBLE THREAT (Book #6)
DOUBLE TARGET (Book #7)

JAKE MERCER THRILLER SERIES
ABSOLUTE THREAT (Book #1)
ABSOLUTE DAMAGE (Book #2)
ABSOLUTE FORCE (Book #3)
ABSOLUTE PERIL (Book #4)
ABSOLUTE TREASON (Book #5)
ABSOLUTE VENGEANCE (Book #6)
ABSOLUTE TARGET (Book #7)

THE SPY GAME
TARGET ONE (Book #1)
TARGET TWO (Book #2)
TARGET THREE (Book #3)
TARGET FOUR (Book #4)
TARGET FIVE (Book #5)
TARGET SIX (Book #6)
TARGET SEVEN (Book #7)
TARGET EIGHT (Book #8)
TARGET NINE (Book #9)
TARGET TEN (Book #10)

TROY STARK THRILLER SERIES
ROGUE FORCE (Book #1)
ROGUE COMMAND (Book #2)
ROGUE TARGET (Book #3)
ROGUE MISSION (Book #4)
ROGUE SHOT (Book #5)

ROGUE STRIKE (Book #6)
ROGUE ORDER (Book #7)

LUKE STONE THRILLER SERIES

ANY MEANS NECESSARY (Book #1)
OATH OF OFFICE (Book #2)
SITUATION ROOM (Book #3)
OPPOSE ANY FOE (Book #4)
PRESIDENT ELECT (Book #5)
OUR SACRED HONOR (Book #6)
HOUSE DIVIDED (Book #7)

FORGING OF LUKE STONE PREQUEL SERIES

PRIMARY TARGET (Book #1)
PRIMARY COMMAND (Book #2)
PRIMARY THREAT (Book #3)
PRIMARY GLORY (Book #4)
PRIMARY VALOR (Book #5)
PRIMARY DUTY (Book #6)

AN AGENT ZERO SPY THRILLER SERIES

AGENT ZERO (Book #1)
TARGET ZERO (Book #2)
HUNTING ZERO (Book #3)
TRAPPING ZERO (Book #4)
FILE ZERO (Book #5)
RECALL ZERO (Book #6)
ASSASSIN ZERO (Book #7)
DECOY ZERO (Book #8)
CHASING ZERO (Book #9)
VENGEANCE ZERO (Book #10)
ZERO ZERO (Book #11)
ABSOLUTE ZERO (Book #12)

Made in the USA
Coppell, TX
12 August 2024

35872033R00090